SEASONS OF CHANGE

When Kathleen Fitzgerald left Ireland twenty years ago, she never planned to return. In England she married firefighter Daniel Jackson and settled down to raise their family. However, when Dan is injured in the line of duty, events have a ripple effect, bringing challenges and new directions to the lives of Dan, Kathleen and their children, as well as Kathleen's parents and her brother, Stephen. How will the members of this extended family cope with their season of change?

*Books by Margaret McDonagh
in the Linford Romance Library:*

HIDDEN LOVE
FULL CIRCLE
SWEET REVENGE
BROKEN HEARTS
FORBIDDEN LOVE
JOURNEY INTO LOVE
SHADOWS OF THE PAST
WEB OF DECEIT
A GAME OF LOVE
CUPID'S ARROW
SHATTERED DREAMS
HER SECRET LEGACY
PORTRAIT OF LOVE

MARGARET McDONAGH

◆

SEASONS OF CHANGE

Complete and Unabridged

LINFORD
Leicester

First published in Great Britain in 2005

First Linford Edition
published 2008

British Library CIP Data

McDonagh, Margaret
    Seasons of change.—Large print ed.—
Linford romance library
1. Love stories
2. Large type books
I. Title
823.9'2 [F]

ISBN 978–1–84782–224–6

Published by
F. A. Thorpe (Publishing)
Anstey, Leicestershire

Set by Words & Graphics Ltd.
Anstey, Leicestershire
Printed and bound in Great Britain by
T. J. International Ltd., Padstow, Cornwall

Acknowledgements

With thanks to:

Sean Buckley, Kevin Caffrey,
Theresa McKenna, Fiona Moran
and Lisa O'Connor in Ireland
for their help with my research queries.

And especially to:

Sarah Quirke, Helen Gee
and all at Ulverscroft
for their support and encouragement.

www.margaretmcdonagh.com

1

Hero

'Ladies and gentlemen, I'm sure you already know why we are gathered here today, but it gives me great pleasure to ask our mayor to say a few words and to present this prestigious award to its most deserving recipient.'

Kathleen Jackson watched as the official speaker stepped back from the microphone on the platform in the town hall assembly room. Behind him sat several dignitaries and the man who was to receive the award — her husband, Dan.

Her heart swelled with pride as she looked at him, resplendent in his uniform, uncomfortable at the fuss being made of him.

Dan smiled as the mayor rose to his feet and nodded to him before stepping forward to the microphone. As he began to speak, indulging in his customary preamble, Kathleen allowed herself a glance around the room.

There were more people here than she would have expected. Some of Dan's old colleagues were present, of course, many of their friends, and a few interested locals.

Members of the district and national press had come and could be seen taking swift shorthand; Kathleen noticed that even the area television station had sent someone. The media interest brought home to her once more just what Dan's award was all about.

Beside her, filled with as much pride as she was, sat their children. Sam, her lanky sixteen-year-old, handsome like his father with the same dark-blond hair and green eyes, shifted uncomfortably in the suit she had insisted he wear for the occasion.

Kathleen smothered a smile as she thought of the kudos his father's celebrity had brought Sam, especially with his girlfriend, Nicola. Dark, petite, and wide-eyed with awe, she sat next to Sam, whispering her comments on the ceremony.

Then there was Laura, pale and thin, with short fair hair and gentle grey-green eyes. Kathleen's daughter was struggling with the throes of adolescence. At fourteen she was turning from an outgoing tomboy into a quiet and withdrawn girl, self-conscious in this kind of crowd. She didn't share Nicola's delight in their surroundings and played nervously with her fingers as she watched the events on stage.

Kathleen looked round as Luke, eight years old and sharing her dark-haired, blue-eyed Celtic colouring, nudged her and grinned. He was almost bursting with excitement that his dad was to be rewarded for his brave actions.

On the other side of her sat James, Luke's twin. They were so alike to look at, but so different in character, Kathleen thought. Swinging his legs and fidgeting, Kathleen knew James couldn't wait to get home and out of his smart clothes. He began to whistle under his breath and Kathleen placed a restraining hand on his arm.

'Hush now, love. Don't spoil your dad's day.'

Sighing, James folded his arms and slumped untidily in his chair. Kathleen turned her attention back to the stage, glad the mayor was at last coming to the point.

'And so, we come to the man himself. A man known to many of us for his long-standing service to the community, a man who made the ultimate sacrifice and placed himself in danger to save the lives of others,' the mayor boomed, his cheeks reddening as he brought his speech to a crescendo.

Catching Laura's gaze, Kathleen exchanged a smile.

'We know the fire service are here to help us in our time of need, but all too often the work these men do is taken for granted and passes unrewarded,' the mayor continued. 'Today, it gives me great pleasure to award one of these brave men a token of appreciation on behalf of our community.

'I'm sure each of you knows Sub Officer Daniel Jackson was seriously injured in the line of duty while saving a young woman and her child from a burning building.

'With no thought for himself, this brave and courageous man led his charges to safety before the roof of the building collapsed on him.'

As the mayor's praise continued, Kathleen noticed Dan shift uncomfortably on his chair.

While she acknowledged her pride in her husband, she knew what he had been through, as a result of his selfless bravery. She certainly wasn't blind to the changes that lay ahead of him. But despite the cost to himself, she knew that Dan would not hesitate to do the same again. That was the kind of man he was, always putting others before himself — compassionate, intelligent, funny and brave. It was why she loved him.

Finally, after what seemed like an age, the mayor turned and gestured to Dan to join him.

'I'll ask Sub Officer Jackson to step forward.'

Kathleen watched tentatively as Dan struggled to his feet, balancing on the sticks he still needed as a result of his injuries. Looking embarrassed, he approached the mayor. Kathleen knew he hated all this fuss, and was uncomfortable being labelled a hero. But that was exactly what he had been. As far as Kathleen was concerned, Dan deserved all the recognition that came his way.

The mayor shook Dan's hand.

'I am delighted to present you with this special award for gallantry, and may I say, on behalf of us all, how proud and grateful we are for your actions.'

'Thank you,' Dan accepted graciously, glancing at the award before slipping it self-consciously into his pocket.

The hall resounded to the applause. Kathleen and the children rose to their feet, huge grins on their faces. Gingerly Dan left the stage, his gait still uncertain as he came across to join them.

Ordeal

'I'm glad that's over,' he muttered, sitting down beside them. 'I didn't think he was ever going to stop.'

'Me, neither!' Luke grinned. 'Can I see the medal, Dad?'

'When we get home, son.'

Wrenching at the knot of his tie, James scuffed the toe of one shoe on the polished wood floor.

'Can we go now?'

'Not just yet.' Kathleen smiled. Her voice was soft with understanding.

'There'll be people who want to talk to your dad. Why don't you go to the buffet table and help yourself to some juice and biscuits?'

The children wandered off towards

the refreshments as the Press descended on Dan. Kathleen sat beside him, knowing what an ordeal this was for him, but proud of the way he was handling it.

'Can you tell us again what happened that evening?' one of the reporters asked.

For the umpteenth time, Dan launched matter of factly into his story, trying unsuccessfully to play down his rôle in the rescue.

Before long, the woman and child he had saved came across to be photographed with him. The young woman, tears of gratitude welling up in her eyes, held the hand of her little girl, who clutched her teddy bear and offered a little posy of flowers to Dan.

It tugged at Kathleen's heart, and she turned away to brush aside a tear of her own.

'You must be very proud of him,' a female reporter from a national paper remarked.

Kathleen smiled.

'Yes. We all are.'

'How is his recovery going?'

'Very well, thank you. But he has a difficult road ahead of him,' Kathleen admitted.

'And what will he do now?' the woman enquired.

Kathleen drew her a sharp glance, aware of the hidden anxieties the reporter had stirred up.

'We're not sure at this point.'

The reporter nodded, frowning down at her notebook.

'But he won't be able to go back to the fire service, will he?'

'No.' Kathleen struggled to maintain her poise. She knew Dan was wearing the uniform that tied him to a job he loved for the last time.

'No, his career there is over. But Dan's a survivor. When he's fit enough, he'll launch himself in a new direction.'

After wishing them well, the reporter moved off, and Kathleen hoped her bold predictions for the future would hold true.

Moving to her husband's side, she

greeted Claire, the woman he had rescued, and her daughter, Megan.

It was obvious Dan was beginning to tire. Reading the signs of his discomfort, Kathleen suggested it was time they made a move.

'Please,' he agreed with a relieved smile. 'I think we can decently slip away now.'

'I'll round up the children.'

Her mission accomplished, they headed towards the door, only to be waylaid by the television crew.

'What are your plans?' a reporter asked, thrusting a microphone under Dan's chin. 'What are you going to do now?'

'Long term, I'm not sure what the future holds,' Dan responded, his smile faltering. 'But for now, we're going to spend Easter with my wife's parents, in Ireland.'

A Fresh Perspective

They had been in Ireland for only a few days and already the peace and beauty of Killarney had worked its magic. Everyone was starting to unwind.

The fabulous views, vigorous walks and generous home-cooked meals had brought colour to their faces and given them all a new bounce and vitality.

Dan, his physical activities restricted, had recovered quickly from the stress of the journey. He was more at ease and comfortable than Kathleen had seen him in ages.

Now, as they walked slowly through the hotel grounds down to the edge of the lough before supper, Kathleen sighed with contentment.

'Happy?' Dan asked.

'Very.' She linked her arm through his. 'Thank you.'

'What for?'

'Making this trip.' She knew the journey had taken its toll on him.

'I wanted to come. I love it here, and I love your family.'

'I know, but . . . '

'Enough,' he chided with a smile, turning her to face him. 'I had

11

reservations, yes, but not about being here, Kath. I've felt better over these last few days than I have since the accident. The children are loving it, too. It's doing us all the world of good.'

Smiling back, Kathleen nodded, resolving not to dwell on things. Here, with spring well advanced, the weather mild and a lush greenness to everything, she felt renewed promise for the future. The peace and beauty of her old home environment had been a comfort, filling her with tranquillity and a sense of hope.

Not that she hadn't had concerns of her own. She couldn't believe how much Killarney had changed since they had last visited. All the new houses and businesses had been a surprise. But the biggest shock had been the state of her parents' hotel.

'Why the frown?' Dan prompted as they sat on a bench by the water's edge.

'I was just thinking about the place. It looks so jaded and neglected. Mam brushed off my concerns and made some lighthearted excuse about the lack of Easter visitors, but I'm still anxious. All is not well.'

Setting his walking-stick aside, Dan took her hand in his.

'You worry too much,' he told her softly.

'I know.'

'Look how you were about Laura before we came away.'

'I know . . . I know, Dan,' she repeated, a new frown creasing the smoothness of her brow. 'She's been more like her old self since we've been here. I was worried. Don't you think she's changed? She's been so quiet and withdrawn lately.'

'Have you talked to her?'

'I tried to. She says she's fine, but . . . Perhaps it's just a stage she's going through?'

'Would you like me to try?'

'I don't know, Dan. I don't want to upset her by dragging the subject up again. I thought I'd play it by ear,' she added uncertainly, 'and wait for her to tell me if anything is bothering her.'

Dan nodded his agreement. He'd been so wrapped up in his own worries that perhaps he hadn't been as observant of his loved ones as he should. But he felt things were changing now. This holiday was giving him a fresh perspective.

As a comfortable silence settled between them, he surveyed his surroundings, admitting how much he loved it here in this small, friendly town with its tranquil lakes and glorious scenery, and the imposing backdrop of McGillicuddy's Reeks.

'I'd forgotten how peaceful this place is,' he confided, adjusting his position to ease his aches. 'It's like another world — fresh, calm, welcoming. I can't imagine why you ever wanted to leave this way of life.'

'As a teenager it just seemed so dull.' Kathleen smiled ruefully, remembering her yearning to get away.

'Maybe.'

She pulled a face at his doubting tone.

'Anyway, if I hadn't gone to London

to do my nursing training, we'd never have met.'

'True,' he conceded. He recalled fondly the day he had first seen her in the casualty department, when she had tended to cuts and bruises he'd sustained during a training mishap.

A laugh bubbled inside her.

'I was so in awe of you — all nervous and tongue-tied!'

'*You* were nervous?' he protested in disbelief. 'I don't know how I ever managed to speak to you! I so nearly didn't ask you out.'

'Was I that unapproachable?'

'I'd just never seen anyone so beautiful.'

'Get away with you, Dan!'

'It's true!' He laughed, amused by the tinge of pink that coloured her cheeks. 'I thought you were bound to have a string of young doctors vying for your attention. Why would you bother with me?'

'Because I thought you were gorgeous! I'd never met anyone like you.'

Drawing her towards him, Dan bent to kiss her, knowing that whatever the future held in store, he was a lucky man to have Kathleen by his side. She was still as beautiful as the day they had met, her blue eyes as vibrant, her hair as dark and silken, soft to his touch.

Kathleen returned his kiss, feeling closer to him and more confident again in their relationship, following the strains of the last few months. They had been through so much together; it could only strengthen their bond.

'Come on.' Dan smiled as he released her and rose gingerly to his feet. 'Let's wander back and find out what havoc our young ones have been causing!'

As the sun began to sink behind the mountains, tinting the sky pale mauve and orange, the colours reflecting on the glinting waters of the lough, Dan and Kathleen strolled hand in hand, enjoying their closeness. The path ahead would not be easy, but they were coming to terms with it now, and

she knew they could weather things
. . . together.

Intrigue

'You're just in time to help me with the
supper!' Mary Fitzgerald greeted her
two eldest grandchildren as they came
into the kitchen.

'Wonderful,' Sam complained with a
hint of sarcasm.

'Don't take any notice of him, Gran.'
Laura smiled. 'He's all grouchy because
he's missing Nicola!'

Sam threw his sister an irritated glare
but refused to rise to the bait.

'What do you want me to do, Gran?'

'Would you be an angel and lay the
guests' tables for me?' Mary asked. 'I've
been that busy this afternoon I'm all
behind. I thought if I got their suppers
out of the way first, we could have an
enjoyable evening to ourselves.'

'Is Uncle Stephen coming with his
girlfriend?' Laura queried, helping Sam

collect cutlery and napkins from the drawers.

'Indeed he is.'

As Laura followed her brother to the guest dining-room, Mary frowned at the thought of Roisin Slattery. She had no intention of sharing her reservations about Stephen's young woman with her grandchildren.

It would be interesting to see what Kathleen made of her brother's companion, Mary thought, busying herself at the stove. Kathleen had never met Roisin, and Mary had kept her comments to herself, not wanting to colour Kathleen's view.

The back door opened, and Mary smiled happily as Kathleen and Dan came in. They looked so much more at ease. She was glad they had decided to make the journey and spend Easter in Ireland.

'Did you enjoy your stroll?'

'It was lovely.' Kathleen grinned. 'Are the others back yet?'

'Sam and Laura are laying tables for

me, but your father and Stephen are not back with the boys yet.'

'Is there anything I can do to help?'

Mary shook her head.

'Sure, you're on holiday! You and Dan help yourself to a drink and relax until supper,' she insisted.

'Did you have a good time in town?' Kathleen asked as Sam and Laura returned to the kitchen.

'It was OK,' Sam admitted grudgingly.

'I enjoyed myself,' Laura chipped in, making a face at her brother. 'Even if old sourpuss here was moody.'

'Shut up, Laura.'

'Sam,' Dan chided, easing himself on to a chair.

'Well, we all know why you're so anxious to get home,' Laura persisted with a teasing grin.

His face darkening, Sam glared again at his sister.

'In case you've forgotten, I have my exams coming up. I'm meant to be studying.'

'You've never seemed so interested in

your course work before,' Kathleen pointed out with an amused smile.

'You and Dad nag me enough about it,' he complained. 'I'll be up in my room until supper.'

As he stomped out, Kathleen exchanged a grin with her husband. Since Sam had met Nicola, his first serious girlfriend, he begrudged all the time he had to spend away from her.

Voices in the hallway announced the arrival of Stephen and Luke. The youngster burst into the kitchen, his face alive with excitement.

'We had a wicked time!' Luke exclaimed. 'We climbed right to the top of the hills, and we saw the deer!'

Full of his adventures, Luke kept them entertained with nonstop chatter. Smiling at his enthusiasm, Kathleen looked across at her brother. She knew how busy he was as a ranger with the National Park Service, but he'd been delighted to take Luke with him that morning, and the outing had clearly been a success.

Tall, dark and undeniably handsome,

her brother was passionate about his work. He was also the most eligible bachelor in the county!

Kathleen was intrigued about the woman he was seeing and couldn't wait to meet her that evening.

'I'll be off,' Stephen announced now, ruffling Luke's hair. 'Roisin and I will be back in an hour or so. Is that OK, Mam?'

'Grand, love.' Mary smiled.

Kathleen said nothing as Stephen left, but she'd noticed her mother's tense expression. More curious than ever, she wondered what Roisin was like.

'As soon as your father gets back with James, I'll serve the guests,' her mother said, glancing at her watch. 'Goodness knows where they've got to, but you know what your da's like when he has the chance to go fishing!'

A Kindred Spirit

'I still haven't caught anything!' James complained after sitting for ages on the bank beside his grandfather. He jiggled the fishing-rod impatiently in his hands.

Kevin Fitzgerald chuckled as he packed away their gear.

'Fishing's not only about catching things.'

'It's not?' James's animated face creased in a frown. 'What's the point of it then?'

'It's about enjoying the environment and the wildlife . . . and having quiet time to think.'

The frown deepened.

'To think about what?'

'Anything!' Kevin tapped out his pipe and slipped it into his pocket. 'I do a lot of my thinking out here.'

'Why?'

'Why not? Don't you ever just like to sit and do nothing?'

James stared in confusion.

'What's the point in doing nothing? There's always too much to do and not enough time to do it in. Mum says I'm always on the go.'

'Does she now!' His grandad laughed,

picked up the rods and began heading back towards the hotel.

'Luke's not, though.' Striving to match his grandfather's stride, James frowned again, as he thought of his more sedate twin. 'He'd probably be the one to sit and do nothing.'

'So didn't you like coming fishing with me?'

'Of course I liked being with you, Gramps, but . . . '

Glancing down at the youngster walking alongside in the gathering dusk, Kevin smiled.

'But what?'

'I wasn't much good at it, was I?'

'You did fine.'

'Luke would be better at it than me.'

'Why do you say that?' Kevin prompted. He saw himself, nearly sixty years ago, in the boy who fidgeted at his side.

James paused for a few moments, glad the fading light hid his expression.

'Luke's better at most things than me,' he confided finally.

'I expect you are good at lots of

things . . . different things. I can teach you to be good at fishing.'

Interest sparked on the young face.

'Really? You'd help me? You think I can do it?'

'Of course you can,' Kevin encouraged, wishing he saw more of his grandchildren. 'I'll bet if you learn the patience of fishing, and the enjoyment of being with your thoughts, you'll be amazed what you can do.'

'When did you learn to fish, Gramps?'

Kevin smiled at the memories.

'I was about your age when my da taught me, here in this very place.

'Just like you, I was so busy rushing around I never stopped to relax and see things — really see things. When I did, it was wonderful!'

As they approached the hotel, James mulled over his grandfather's words. He was unable to explain why he felt so close to this man, whom he so rarely saw, but he did.

It was as if he had found a kindred spirit. He wanted to be like him — to make him proud.

'Will you really teach me, Gramps?'

'I'd be delighted.'

Stowing the fishing equipment in the shed, Kevin locked the door and turned to his grandson.

'It can be our special time alone together. Deal?'

The promise brought a huge grin to James's face.

'Deal!' he echoed, and they shook hands solemnly, sealing their new bond.

'Come on, now. We'd best get in or your gran will tan my hide for being late for supper!'

Laughing together, they walked towards the light that spilled from the kitchen door.

Stylish

After a shower and a change of clothes, Stephen let himself out of his cottage on the outskirts of town and drove to pick up Roisin.

It had been a great day with Luke in the National Park. His nephew was interested in everything, and keen to learn. And he was smart, too, asking all kinds of questions!

Stephen really enjoyed the variety his job afforded him. One day he'd be out on the hills counting the deer, the next clearing the invasive plants that threatened to swamp the natural vegetation, the one after giving a talk at a school, or taking a party round the Park.

Being a ranger was all he had ever wanted, and since he had been Luke's age, he'd hung around the Park, learning and volunteering . . . probably making a real nuisance of himself. He grinned at the memory. But his keenness had paid off. He'd worked hard, and when a job had become available, he'd been the natural choice.

Drawing the car to a halt outside Roisin's flat, he stepped out and rang the doorbell.

'She'll be right down,' her flatmate announced through the entry intercom.

Retreating to the car, Stephen leaned on the bonnet to wait. The evening air was cooling, but he'd seen the first bats of the year on the wing just a few days before — another sign that spring was advancing and summer not far away.

He loved all the little signs in the flora and fauna that marked the changing of the seasons.

'Hi!' Roisin closed the door and walked towards him, her high-heels tapping a tattoo on the pavement.

'You look grand.' Stephen smiled, admiring the slender figure in the simple but stylish black dress.

'Thank you. Mind the lipstick.' She turned her face so his kiss landed on her cheek. 'Are we late?'

Slightly miffed, Stephen shook his head.

'No, Mam's seeing to the guests first.'

Once in the car, Stephen watched out of the corner of his eye as Roisin checked her makeup. Everything about her was perfect — the stylish cut of her shining auburn hair, her subtly made-up face with its delicate nose, slanting green eyes and determined chin.

She was a very beautiful woman, classy and confident. But she could also be incredibly single-minded. Stephen had been on the sharp end of her tongue more than once in their six-month relationship.

'Did you have a good day at work?' he asked.

'Great!' She grinned across at him, dabbing a touch of perfume behind her ears. 'I'll tell you about it later.'

'I spent the day with Luke. He came with me to the Park. He was into everything! He reminded me of me at the same age,' he told her, smiling reminiscently.

'Not the Park now, Stephen,' she scolded lightly, failing to mask the exasperation behind her words.

As he turned into the drive of the hotel, Stephen hid his own dart of irritation. Roisin made no secret of the fact that his work bored her, yet he was constantly expected to take an interest in her up-and-coming career with the bank.

Now, as they entered the family's private part of the hotel building, Stephen just hoped that Roisin would enjoy the evening and make a good impression. If she would only keep her insensitive comments about the run-down state of his parents' business to herself, he was sure the meal would go smoothly.

★　　★　　★

'And what exactly do you do, Kathleen?' Roisin asked, her smile failing to reach her eyes.

Kathleen's own smile was strained.

'I'm a nurse.'

'Oh, I see. How interesting.'

It was quite clear from the younger woman's voice that she found nursing anything but interesting. Kathleen hung on to her temper with difficulty. Only an understanding squeeze of the hand from Dan helped her maintain her composure.

From the moment they had arrived, Roisin had managed to convey her disdain for the hotel and just about everyone in it, while seeming to ooze charm. Kathleen was not fooled. What on earth did her brother see in this woman?

'I find it very interesting,' she countered now. 'And extremely reward-ing.'

'Of course. No doubt the money is a big help — now Dan can't work.'

There it was again, Kathleen fumed, the put-down. It had been the same all through dinner.

Ambition

Kathleen grabbed a quiet moment with her mother in the kitchen.

'You never said what she was like. Is she always so arrogant?'

Mary grimaced.

'I thought it was just me — not that your da is keen.'

'I'm not surprised!'

'Your brother likes her. That's what matters to us.'

Unconvinced, Kathleen shook her head. There was no point going on at her mother about it.

'Mum, is it OK if we go upstairs now?' Sam asked from the kitchen doorway.

'Of course.' She smiled, seeing the others grouped behind them. 'Do you lot want any drinks to take up with you?'

She busied herself with glasses of soft drinks, then ushered the children upstairs.

'I'll come up and see you shortly,' she promised.

As they clattered up the stairs, she heard their fading voices reaching back to her down the passageway.

'What does Uncle Stephen see in her?' Laura exclaimed. 'She's dreadful! Who does she think she is, looking down her nose at us?'

'It's a very pretty nose,' Sam chipped in, and they all laughed.

Stifling a smile, Kathleen took a deep breath and joined the adults for coffee.

'And today I was offered a promotion. A big job at the head office in Dublin!' Roisin was finishing. Kathleen poured herself a coffee and sat down beside Dan.

'Congratulations,' Mary praised politely. 'You certainly work very hard.'

'It's the only way to get on, and I'm very ambitious,' Roisin confirmed, smiling at Stephen.

Kathleen realised from the expression on her brother's face that this was the first he had heard of the promotion. And he didn't look happy about it.

As much as she tried to make allowances for Roisin's behaviour, she couldn't help but wonder why the younger woman had chosen to make her announcement in such a boastful way, rather than talking with Stephen first. Clearly, her brother was wondering the same.

'Why didn't you tell me about the job?' Stephen asked when they left a little while later. He revved the engine with unnecessary force as he drove towards the gateway.

'I only heard today.' Roisin pouted. 'What's the big deal?'

'You're leaving for Dublin. How did you expect me to feel?'

Roisin gave an impatient sigh.

'I thought you'd be really pleased. It'll be great for us, a real move up in the world.'

'Us?' Stephen challenged, a frown on his face as he drew up outside Roisin's flat. The glow of a streetlight illuminated the inside of the car.

'Of course! I want you to come with me. We can start a whole new life.'

'I don't want a whole new life, Roisin. I'm happy with the one I have,' he pointed out with a flash of irritation.

Roisin gave a condescending laugh.

'Oh, Stephen! You could be so much

more than a ranger. In Dublin we'll have all kinds of opportunities. We can really go places.'

'Being a ranger is all I want to be, Roisin.'

'Well, I want more for us even if you don't,' she argued. 'Your sister escaped this town and went to London! It's a shame she just ended up being a nurse and doing the family thing.'

Stephen felt his temper rise.

'There's nothing wrong with Kathleen's career, or her family. And there's nothing wrong with living here.'

'There is for me.'

'And if I don't want you to go?'

'I won't let anyone hold me back, Stephen,' she told him, her expression hard and determined. 'I care about you and I want us to be together, but in Dublin, not here.'

'I'm not giving up my job or my family.'

'If you loved me you'd come with me.'

He shook his head, angry and sad at the same time.

'If you loved me we'd have discussed this before you made your decision. Love is about sharing, Roisin, not just about getting your own way.'

'Then you have your way and I'll have mine,' she retorted, her eyes glittering angrily. She opened the door and stepped out on to the pavement.

'I want this chance, Stephen. Either you come with me or it's over between us!'

Making Plans

The Easter weekend had been really enjoyable and the family had shared in the lovely service in the cathedral on Sunday morning.

Now, several days later, the end of their holiday had arrived all too soon. Kathleen felt sad that they would be leaving the next day. She hadn't enjoyed Ireland so much in years. It had been perfect, and just what they had needed. It would be hard to say goodbye to her parents and Stephen and return to England.

Tonight was to be their last family dinner together. Rounding up the children, she made sure James and Luke had cleaned up properly after their romp in the woods, and helped her mother carry the meal through to the family dining-room.

The chat was happy and full of laughter, but Kathleen couldn't help glimpsing a shadow in Stephen's eyes. Roisin was noticeable by her absence, and Kathleen wondered what had happened between them the week before. Her brother had been silent on the subject, but it was clear something was bothering him.

After a wonderful meal, they adjourned to the living-room, to relax with coffee.

'It's been grand having you all here,' her father announced. 'As it's your last night, and while we're all together, your mam and I feel we ought to tell you of the plans we've been making and what we've decided to do.'

Surprised, Kathleen glanced at Stephen, but it was clear from the puzzled frown on his face that he was as much in the dark as she was.

'Decisions about what?' Stephen asked, setting down his glass and leaning forward.

Bombshell

Kathleen noticed her parents exchange a glance before her father cleared his throat and continued speaking.

'Your mam and I are both getting on in years and we've started to think about the future,' he admitted, reaching out to take Mary's hand in his. 'We're finding things a bit of a struggle here.'

'You're not ill or anything?' Kathleen asked, worry building inside her.

'We're both fine, pet,' her mother reassured her with a smile. 'It's not even the money. But . . . truth be told, we've both lost our enthusiasm. We don't have the energy we once had, or the desire, to modernise the building and keep things going.'

Kevin nodded his agreement.

'I know you've noticed how run-down the place is looking. It really needs some young blood, someone with the will, energy and determination to bring in fresh ideas.'

'I thought the hotel business was booming around here,' Stephen commented, concern in his eyes.

'Indeed it is. In fact, that's one of the reasons we've given this so much thought,' Mary admitted. 'It seems the time is right now.'

In the short silence that followed, Kathleen experienced a shiver of unease.

'The time is right for what?'

'Your mam and I have made some enquiries. We're spent ages talking it over. It wasn't an easy decision to make, right enough,' her father confided, pausing for a moment before dropping his final bombshell.

'We waited until we could tell you all

in person. This is going to be our last season running the hotel. We're putting the property on the market.'

Scarcely aware of the stunned silence that gripped all those in the room, Kathleen stared at her parents in shocked amazement.

'You're selling? Seriously? But I didn't realise you were feeling like this. What will you do?'

The questions came tumbling out and everyone began talking at once. The children were upset and confused. Dan tried to calm them down, reasoning out their concerns. Stephen was as shocked as Kathleen, who slumped in her seat, unable to believe it.

But why was it such a shock? After all, hadn't she noticed the signs of her parents slowing down?

And it wasn't as if she lived here, she told herself. She really had no say in what happened to the old place.

It was just that, presented with the cold reality, she realised how much she loved her old home, how she relied on it being her port in a storm, familiar and dependable.

As the surprised and curious chatter abated, her parents answered some of the bombardment of questions.

'Neither you nor Kathleen have ever been that interested in the business, Stephen,' Mary pointed out. 'You both have your careers and commitments, and your da and I never expected either of you to forgo your choices to help us out.'

'That's right,' Kevin agreed. 'The hotel has kept this family going all these years, but we don't feel too much sadness at the prospect of leaving.

'Apart from the memories, of course, but we'll take those with us,' he finished, a familiar twinkle in his kindly blue eyes.

'As for what we'll do,' Mary chipped in, 'we've seen this grand bungalow up at Aghadoe Heights, with wonderful views of the Reeks and the lough. It will suit us fine for our retirement.

'We'll have our friends about us,

Stephen close by, and we'll have more time for you and your family, Kathleen.'

'You can spend as much time as you like here with us, of course, but we'll be able to visit England more, too,' her father added, winking at James.

Excited by the prospect, the children hugged their grandparents. Kathleen envied them their casual acceptance of the circumstances. She herself was struggling to come to terms with the fact.

Meeting Dan's gaze, she tried to smile. Seeing the understanding and concern in his eyes, she began to well up.

Excusing herself, she left the room and went outside, the night air cool, the sky clear, the velvet blackness filled with stars.

Sitting on a seat in the garden, the Reeks silhouetted as they loomed above the glinting waters of the lough, Kathleen pondered her reaction.

Why had the idea of the loss of the hotel shaken her so deeply?

'Are you OK?'

The sound of Dan's voice startled Kathleen, but she nodded as he joined her, and shifted along the seat to make room for him. He sat close, subconsciously rubbing a little at the pain in his back.

Glancing at his profile in the moonlight, she saw he was absorbed in thought.

'I just had no idea this was in the wind,' she confided after a few moments, needing to break the silence and share her anxieties. 'I was worried about how run-down things were looking, but I never expected this.'

As she shivered, Dan slid his arm around her shoulders, drawing her against him.

'It's really upset you, hasn't it?'

'I know it's silly. I don't even live here.' She tried to laugh it off, but her voice was husky with emotion. 'It's not the hotel itself, the business part, it's the place . . . knowing it's always here . . . part of me and my past.

'I never expected to feel this strongly, Dan. But being here this Easter has made me realise how much I still love it — and how much I'll miss it. The thought of it changing just hit me — especially on top of everything else that's happened. The future seems so uncertain at the moment.'

'It's only natural,' he said, attempting to reassure her. 'It was bound to be a shock, coming out of the blue as it did. Even Stephen had no idea, and he's on the doorstep.'

'I know.'

'I understand how you feel, sweetheart. It's your childhood home, part of you, and you feel you've lost it. Just like me — I feel I've lost part of me, too. All I ever wanted was to be a fireman.'

Returning his embrace, Kathleen ached for him.

'Oh . . . Dan . . . I'm so sorry.'

'It's all right.' His fingers stroked the softness of her tearstained cheek. 'Your parents seem to have thought it all through, anyway.'

'But why can't they just keep the house and give up the business side?' She looked up at him, seeking reassurance.

'It's far too big for them to rattle around in on their own. How would they keep it going with no money coming in?'

Kathleen hated to admit he was right.

'I suppose so. It does seem to need a lot of work doing to it.'

She lapsed into silence. The shock announcement had wiped the gloss from her holiday.

'Too much is changing, Dan. Who knows what's in store for us?'

'Think About It'

Dan hesitated, unsure how to voice the idea taking shape in his head. It was crazy — impulsive — but the more he thought about it, the more excited he felt. It could be the answer to their prayers.

'What is it?' she asked, sensing his restlessness.

Dan took a deep breath and turned to face her in the moonlight.

'While you were all talking in there, about your parents' plans, I was thinking . . . '

'About what?'

'Us . . . our future . . . the hotel.'

Her eyes glinted as she looked at him.

'What do you mean?'

'Why don't we buy out your parents and move here? We could take over running the hotel?'

Kathleen pulled away from him in shock.

'Dan, you're not serious?'

'I am, Kath, very serious.'

'But how can we? Think what such a move would mean! There are the children to think about, and Sam's exams. And what about my job?' she added, running through all the problems that cascaded around her mind.

'Not to mention your health. I know you've come on leaps and bounds, but are you strong enough to take on such a project?'

Disappointment swept over him at her protests. In the short time he had considered the proposal, he had convinced himself he could make it work. How could he persuade her?

'I may not be strong enough now, Kath, but I will be. Besides it wouldn't happen overnight.'

'But . . . '

'At least think about it,' he cajoled, taking her hands in his. 'We all love it here. You just said yourself how much you'll miss it. We know we have changes to face. I have to find something I'm capable of earning a living at; something to believe in.

'This could be the opportunity we need — a new beginning for the whole family . . .'

2

Time To Talk

Having dropped James and Luke off at school and struggled round the supermarket for the weekly shop, Kathleen headed home to enjoy the rest of her day off. The weather was beautiful, the sun shone in a cloudless clear blue sky, and the air was pleasingly fresh.

The shopping stowed away, Kathleen switched on the kettle, then went out of the back door and down the narrow garden path to the large shed Dan used as a workshop.

As she had expected, Dan was concentrating on his latest carving. He had always been good with his hands, and during his convalescence was taking solace in working with wood, making studies of birds and animals, and carving nick-nacks for the children.

'Hi,' she said softly, alerting him to her presence.

'Hi, yourself!' His green eyes crinkled at the corners as he smiled, drawing her close for a kiss. 'Is that the shopping all done? I'm sorry I'm not more help to you, love.'

'Don't be daft. You're doing fine. I've just put the kettle on. Do you fancy a coffee?'

'I'd love one, thanks.'

Kathleen dropped a kiss on the top of his head. Even after all these years his presence still made her tummy flutter.

'Will you come indoors?' she asked now. 'We so rarely get the house to ourselves.

'I've been thinking over what you said about Ireland. I'd like to talk.'

Hope flared in Dan's eyes at her suggestion as he struggled to his feet and followed her into the house. The time had flown by since their return from Killarney, and opportunities to discuss Dan's idea had been few and far between.

48

The coffee made, they wandered through to the living-room. Kathleen opened the glass doors leading out on to the patio and stood for a moment letting the scents from the garden soothe her while she collected her thoughts. She could feel Dan's presence behind her, watching her, second-guessing what she was about to say.

'Kath . . . '

'Dan . . . '

They both spoke at once, then stopped, laughing nervously at each other.

'Go ahead,' Dan said, as they turned to face each other.

'I have so many mixed feelings about the idea of moving,' she admitted after a moment, unsure how to voice her anxieties. 'I was so surprised at first. I didn't mean to hurt you by being dismissive. Things have been hard for you, I know.'

'I've been thinking a lot about it, too. And I feel more determined than ever, Kath.'

'But how could it ever work?' she asked.

Dan visibly relaxed.

'Let me tell you my plans.'

Kathleen listened as he outlined his detailed ideas for moving and taking over the hotel. He certainly seemed to have covered all his bases, she acknowledged.

'I'm sure we could manage financially,' he was saying now. 'We'll get a very good price for this house. It's risen dramatically in value since we moved in all those years ago. Now would be an excellent time to sell. There's not much of the mortgage left to pay off. Then there are the savings we've managed to stash away, and we still have insurance and compensation to come from the accident.'

Kathleen nodded, trying to grasp all the implications.

'But it's not just the money, Dan.'

'I know. We have to consider the children, too.'

'I can't imagine how they'll react.

Laura is so difficult at the moment. She's become completely withdrawn again since Easter. And it's only a couple of years until her GCSEs.'

'She's a very bright girl, Kathleen. I'm sure she would manage,' Dan pointed out. 'And the twins are adaptable. Luke's still mad keen on the National Park; he speaks about little other than being a ranger. And James seems to have really taken to your father.'

Kathleen smiled, admitting the truth of her husband's remarks.

'A change of environment may be good for them,' Dan suggested.

It was a reasonable point. She had little doubt that her robust and resilient boys would adapt to almost anything. And being closer to their grandparents and uncle could only be good for them.

She frowned then, thinking of their eldest son.

'What of Sam?'

'He'll have his own opinion. He's almost a man now, Kath.'

'Or he likes to think he is. He'd hate moving to Ireland. Dan. He's had such a struggle with these GCSEs; he wouldn't want to adapt to a different system. And all his friends are here: that's not to mention Nicola, sport, and his part-time job.'

'And what about you?' Dan asked, zeroing in on the nub of her indecision.

'What do you really want?'

She shook her head, not knowing how to voice the welter of emotions inside her.

'The whole idea is crazy! We must be mad to be thinking of it!' she protested, waving her arms in confusion.

Dan stilled her agitation, clasping her hands gently in his.

'I know it's scary. It's a huge upheaval, but what else is there for me, Kath?'

Convinced

Surprised at the emotion in his voice, Kathleen met Dan's troubled gaze.

'Look, I know you aren't happy in your job. You didn't want to go back into nursing. I know you only did it because you had to. Do you really want to go on working at the surgery until you retire?'

'No,' she admitted. It was true — she was disenchanted with the NHS.

'Professionally I'll never again be able to do what I trained for. The fire service is over for me. But I'm only forty, Kath. I don't want to end up on the scrapheap.

'This is a huge opportunity for us — all of us.'

Kathleen pondered his words. She could hear his frustration. He hadn't shown this much enthusiasm for anything since the accident.

'You're right.'

'Pardon?'

'You're right. It is an incredible chance. I've been too caught up in my worries. I was shocked and sad when Mum and Dad talked of selling up. I suppose I found the consequences too frightening to admit how much I secretly wished we could go for it.'

'You did? . . . I mean, you do?

'You're not just saying that, are you. Kathleen?' Dan demanded.

'I wasn't prepared to consider the idea. because although I yearned for it, there seemed to be too many obstacles in the way.'

'Obstacles can be overcome.'

'I know. You've convinced me. Dan.' She shook her head, smiling at the eagerness on his face.

'We must be mad! So where do we go from here?' she asked, barely stopping to take in the life-changing events they had just set in motion.

'We'll have to talk to the children, and my parents, and . . . '

Dan laughed, halting her rush of words.

'Hold on! One step at a time.

'I have my visit to the consultant in a couple of days. I suggest we see what he has to say before we finally commit ourselves. If I get the all clear, we'll approach your parents and tackle the children. How does that sound?'

Feeling almost heady with nervous excitement, Kathleen agreed.

'It's Right For Me'

'How did you get on?' Sam called. He struck a pose against the school railing as he waited for Nicola to cross the yard.

He had finished his last exam that lunchtime, but his girlfriend still had a couple more to go, not least the chemistry one she had just finished.

'OK, I think. It was easier than I expected.'

'I don't know how you can do it,' he exclaimed in admiration. He carried her bag along with his own and took her hand in his.

'How about you?'

Sam grimaced, remembering the struggle he'd had with the geography paper that morning.

'So-so. I'm just relieved it's all over.'

As they walked companionably to the bus stop, Sam reflected that he wouldn't have survived these exams without Nicola's support. She was so smart, and had been really patient, helping him through his revision.

'What did you do this afternoon?' Nicola asked as they sat on a wall, waiting for the bus. Her dark hair gleamed in the sunshine.

Slipping his arm around her slender frame, Sam grinned, unable to withhold his news another moment.

'I called in at the garage to see Brian,' he admitted, his bubbling excitement finally given rein.

'And?'

'He's offered me a permanent place! A proper apprenticeship with a guaranteed job at the end of it!'

'Sam! That's brilliant!' Nicola enthused, hugging him. 'I'm so proud of you.'

'I was desperate for it to be OK. It's been really good working there at weekends and in the holidays. I just know it's right for me, Nic.

'And if Brian expands his racing enterprise, I may be able to get experience working round the tracks!'

Nicola's hazel eyes shone with excitement.

'That's so cool, Sam.'

The bus came and they chatted about Sam's plans on the journey to the stop outside her house. Once there, they lingered in the kitchen over fruit juice and flapjacks.

'Enough about me.' Sam laughed. 'Have you much work to do for your final exams tomorrow?'

'A bit. I'm really nervous.'

'You'll be fine. You're not thick like me!'

'Don't say that, Sam. You're not thick. You're kind and caring. We're just good at different things. There's more to life than swotting over formulae and anatomy!'

Sam, too happy to be down for long, smiled back.

'Any news of your summer placement?'

'Yes, didn't I tell you? I had a letter this morning and they are definitely going to offer me a chance to work there for the holidays,' Nicola confirmed happily.

'That's great!'

Nicola's driving ambition was to be a vet. Sam knew how much she wanted the valuable experience she would gain while she waited to take her A-levels and sort out a place at veterinary college.

'I bet your parents are pleased,' he added.

'Yeah, they're OK about it. What about you? Have you told your family about the apprenticeship?'

'No.' Sam looked away, stubborn and defiant.

'Not yet. They'll just go on about me staying on at school or going to college. But I just know this job is right for me. They'll see that for themselves when my GCSE results come in.'

Nicola hesitated, knowing how touchy he was about the aspirations his parents had for him. She sometimes envied him his chaotic family; it could be lonely being an only child with career-minded parents, who were frequently late home. Sam's house was always a flurry of noise and activity.

'I'd better let you get on with your revision,' Sam decided, rising reluctantly.

'One more night and it'll be all over — for a while.'

'I'll meet you on the bus in the morning,' he promised, drawing her to him and kissing her goodbye.

She kissed him back, sorry to see him go, torn between the need to pass her exams and her yearning to have fun. She watched from the window as he walked down the path and disappeared behind the hedge.

She'd been over the moon when he'd asked her out! All the girls at school were crazy about Sam. He was good-looking, tall and athletic — and he'd picked her! Now, with his apprenticeship and her placement, it looked like everything was coming together.

★ ★ ★

'So there we have it,' Mr Hobson concluded, pushing his spectacles higher up his nose and peering across the desk. 'We've reached the stage where there is nothing more we can do for you. Have you anything you'd like to ask?'

Small, greying and with a sharp, blue gaze, the consultant was brisk and straightforward. Dan endeavoured to assimilate his summing up, while beside him, staunch in her support, Kathleen squeezed his hand.

'Won't there be any improvement?' he asked at last.

'There's always hope, Dan. I'm sure that with time you'll learn to adjust.'

Dan nodded slowly. He had never expected a miracle, but learning his body might make no further progress was still a blow. Glancing at Kathleen, he registered the sympathy in her eyes. He faced Mr Hobson again.

'So how much can I do?'

'That largely depends on you; on how you feel. You have to find your own level and discover how far you can push yourself.'

The doctor paused, steepling his hands under his chin.

'You are a young man, Dan. There's still a great life ahead of you.

'Have you any plans?'

'I didn't have until recently,' Dan admitted, pausing to glance at Kathleen.

Smiling, she addressed the consultant.

'My parents own a small hotel in Ireland. I was raised there. They are retiring soon, and Dan and I have been considering the possibility of moving, and taking over the hotel,' she explained. 'I'm concerned how much Dan will be able to do — in a physical sense, you understand.'

'Well, as I said, the physical aspect is something you'll have to discover for yourself. But I think that's an excellent idea.'

'You do?' Dan responded, surprised at Mr Hobson's ready encouragement.

'Absolutely,' the older man enthused. 'I see no reason to advise against such a move.'

Dan burned with enthusiasm. He wasn't finished; he could make a future for his family.

Kathleen's Decision

As they left the consulting room and walked slowly to the carpark, both he and Kathleen were lost in thought.

The silence stretched on the journey home. He wondered if she was having second thoughts about the move.

Once indoors, Kathleen made tea and carried it through to the sitting-room. Dan looked pale after his afternoon's ordeal.

'Are you OK?' she asked, sitting beside him.

'I really want to do this, Kath — more than ever. But I need to know it's what you want, too.'

She was silent for a moment, gathering her thoughts.

'That's the crazy thing.' She smiled.

'What is?'

'The whole time I was growing up I couldn't wait to get away. There was no way I was ever going to be tied down, working in the hotel! And now . . . '

She broke off, taking his hand in hers, smiling at his anxious expression.

'Now?' he probed.

'The idea of it being sold to someone else fills me with dread. It's a mad idea, Dan, but I'm up for it!'

Dan laughed in delight, drawing her to him.

'Thank you,' he whispered huskily.

'Don't thank me yet.' Kathleen laughed when he released her. 'We still have to tell the children.'

'Well, there's no time like the present.' Dan beamed happily. 'Laura and the twins will be home soon.'

'And Sam? Should we wait until Friday when he comes back from his cricket trip?'

Dan frowned.

'I don't see why we can't sound the others out first. Sam's always difficult to pin down — he's never in.'

'All right.' Kathleen nodded, still uncertain. 'I suppose it may be better to talk to him alone, anyway.'

Something To Discuss

The decision made, they waited for the three younger children to come home, tension and anticipation mounting with each passing moment. Finally, the door banged and the boys' lively chatter filled the hall. Laura followed quietly in their wake.

'Thanks for seeing them home, love.' Kathleen smiled at her daughter as she came into the sitting-room. 'Good day?'

Laura scowled and shrugged non-committally.

'Same as usual. Did you get on OK, Dad?'

'Fine, poppet, thanks. Boys,' Dan called as they dumped their bags noisily in the kitchen and raided the fridge, 'come in here, please. Will you stay, too, Laura? Your mother and I have something to discuss with you all.'

The twins quickly organised their milk and biscuits and sat on the floor in front of their dad. Laura sank warily on to a chair, her gaze lowered. Kathleen exchanged a worried glance with Dan. This strangeness in their daughter was the next thing they would have to tackle.

'James was told off again in class.' Luke grinned.

'Was not!'

James, who hadn't bothered to remove his school shoes, aimed a swift, sharp kick at his brother's shin.

'Just 'cos you're a goody two shoes.'

'That's enough, both of you,' Dan asserted.

The twins glowered at each other, fists clenched.

'Your father was signed off by the consultant today,' Kathleen announced. 'We've been talking about the future. You know that Dad will have to find another job. So we've had an idea and we want to know what you think.'

'What sort of idea?' the twins asked in unison.

Taking a deep breath, Dan began to speak.

'I'm not going to be able to be a fireman any more, but I want to do something interesting. Do you remember your grandparents talking about selling the hotel, when we were there at Easter?'

The three youngsters nodded, varying degrees of disappointment on their faces.

'Well,' Dan continued, 'your mother and I think it would be an excellent idea if we moved there and took over running the hotel ourselves. What do you think?'

'Are you serious?' Laura whispered, dumbstruck.

Unsure what reaction was to follow, Kathleen nodded.

'Laura . . . ' she began, only to be interrupted by the twins.

'Yes!' James exploded, leaping to his feet and running round the room. 'Yes, yes, yes! We're going to Ireland! We're going to Ireland!'

Usually more subdued than his twin, Luke joined the excited dance.

'Yippee! I'm going to be a ranger!'

Dan couldn't help but laugh in relief at the exuberant reaction to the news. He had expected his children to be adaptable, but hadn't anticipated their euphoria.

He looked at his daughter. A rare smile split her face, though she seemed on the brink of tears.

'Laura? What do you think?' he asked with concern, sending Kathleen a quick glance.

'Can we really go?'

'We certainly plan to.' Kathleen smiled, surprised by the young girl's emotional reaction. 'Would you like to move there?'

'I'd love it, Mum,' she confirmed with uncharacteristic positiveness. 'I'd really love it!'

The evening passed in a happy whirl of plans and ideas. Laura was more animated than Kathleen had seen her in ages. It was wonderful to hear her laugh again.

'I can't believe how well that went!' Dan exclaimed when the children had finally settled down and gone to bed.

'I know!' Kathleen grinned. 'It was great to see them so excited, especially Laura.'

'There's still Sam to consider.'

'Yes.' She sobered for a moment; wondering if her eldest son would be so enthusiastic about the move. 'He'll be home in a couple of days and then I can ring my parents and make some arrangements!'

Problems

Kathleen found it hard to concentrate on her work at the surgery. Her mind was filled with the children's reactions to the announcement two days ago and her own excitement at the prospect of returning to Ireland. She had never realised the lingering homesickness lurking within her.

She helped her final patient of the morning from the treatment room, and sat down to write up her notes. The telephone buzzed.

'Yes, Carol? Don't tell me there's a latecomer. I was just looking forward to my lunch!'

'No, don't worry!' the receptionist answered. 'It's Dan on the phone for you. I'll put him through.'

As soon as she heard her husband's voice Kathleen knew that something was wrong.

'What is it?' she asked.

'The school have just rung. It's Laura.'

Kathleen's stomach lurched.

'What about her? What's wrong? Dan, is she hurt?'

'No. Kath, it's nothing like that. They want to know why she's not at school,' Dan told her, his voice puzzled and concerned.

'But she is!' Kathleen exclaimed. 'I dropped her off myself!'

'No-one has seen her. Apparently, this isn't the first time she's skipped classes.'

'I'm coming home,' Kathleen announced, balancing the phone between her ear and shoulder as she started to gather her belongings.

'If she's not at school, Dan, then where on earth is she?'

★ ★ ★

'Did you hear about the student?' Pat, one of his fellow park rangers, asked Stephen as they returned to the centre in the late afternoon.

'What student?'

'From Canada — for a year's

placement. She arrives next month according to the official missive,' Pat continued with a grin. He poured a mug of tea from the pot he'd just made and handed it to Stephen.

Stephen took the mug with a grateful smile.

'Thanks. I thought the powers-that-be were cutting back on placements?'

'There you go. It shows what we know!'

Smothering a groan, Stephen took his mug and sat down at one of the desks, pushing a pile of paperwork out of the way.

He hoped this student would be better than the last one. The rangers had spent more time babysitting and getting the young man out of scrapes than concentrating on their work!

Finishing his tea, Stephen filled in some of his paperwork in the half-hour before he went home. The room hummed with a gentle background chatter as other staff came and went. Finally, he pushed his work aside and rose to his feet.

'Are you off home?' Pat asked.

'It's a shame the delectable Roisin won't be waiting for you!' one of the other rangers teased.

Stephen smiled, but their good-natured banter brought home to him Roisin's absence. The gulf between them after her shock announcement at Easter had been unbridgeable. After several more arguments, designed to make him feel guilty for his refusal to abandon life in Killarney, they had decided to call it a day.

Roisin had disappeared out of his life to climb the bank's career ladder in Dublin.

Perhaps it was for the best, he allowed. The lure of Dublin had been stronger than her feelings for him. He would just have to accept that and move on.

Next day, with some free hours to fill and feeling at a loose end, he headed over to visit his parents. He pulled up in front of the hotel, wondering why he hadn't noticed its dilapidated appearance until it had been pointed out. Guilt niggled at him — he should have been more observant of his parents' needs.

The news that they planned to sell up had been as much of a shock to him as to his sister, despite his proximity.

He went in the kitchen door and found his mother surprisingly twitchy and fussing around.

'Stephen!' She gave him a quick hug before flitting away again, glancing intermittently at the door that led to the hotel dining-room. 'I wasn't expecting you.'

'I thought I'd drop by as I had some time off. Are you OK?' he asked with a frown, realising she wasn't really listening to him.

'Mmmm? Sorry, what did you say?'

Stephen laughed, bemused at her behaviour.

'What's going on, Mam?'

'Oh! Well, you see, your da is showing a prospective buyer round the place!' Mary explained, her voice filled with nervous excitement.

'Already?'

'I know! We couldn't believe it. Your da only spoke with the agent a couple of weeks ago. We never expected things to move so soon, but they rang yesterday and said they had an interested party!'

Helping himself to a cup of coffee from the pot, Stephen sat at the table and pondered his feelings on the sale of the hotel. He was pleased for his parents if this was what they wanted, but, like his sister, he regretted the imminent loss of a place that had always been home. Not that he'd ever been interested in running it.

'Is this really what you want?' he asked, seeking reassurance as his mother joined him at the table, fidgeting with some menus.

'Goodness, yes! We've had a good life here, sure enough, but the time has come for us to do what we want for a change.'

'I didn't realise you felt so tied down, so tired of the place.'

His mother tutted.

'And why should you? Neither your

da nor I expected you or Kathleen to take over. You have your own lives.

'I have to ask you, Stephen . . . about Roisin . . . are you . . . Do you think you'll be OK?'

'I'll be fine, Mam. Roisin made her choice. I made mine. Dublin's not for me.'

'Good. That's good, son.' She smiled distractedly.

At least his mother was too preoccupied to give him the 'plenty more fish in the sea' speech. Stephen smiled to himself, remembering her clumsy attempts at raising his spirits after past break-ups.

Time For A Change

He was about to speak again when the door opened and his father came in, a broad grin on his face.

'How did it go, Kevin?' Mary asked, jumping to her feet and hurrying across to him.

'Grand, grand,' he reassured her, all the time rubbing his hands together in satisfaction. 'Sure, he was taken with the place, right enough.'

'And will he make an offer, do you think?'

Kevin put an arm around his wife's shoulders and hugged her to him.

'I reckon he will — a good one, too.'

'Stephen, isn't that wonderful?' His mother beamed. 'It's all so exciting! I must ring Kathleen and tell her the good news.'

'Why not wait until you're sure?' Stephen cautioned, wondering if his sister was feeling similarly emotional.

His father nodded.

'Perhaps he's right, Mary.'

'You men! Always ones to put a damper on things.

'It's all working out far better than I'd ever hoped, Kevin. At this rate, we'll be set for our new life by Christmas!'

3

Where's Laura?

'I'm sorry I've been so long, Dan.' Kathleen burst through the door in breathless apology.

'I was wondering what had happened to you,' Dan admitted. 'I've made tea if you want some. And I've rung round Laura's friends, but the parents who are in couldn't help me. It seems no-one has seen her for a while.'

Kathleen accepted a cup of tea and sat down at the kitchen table.

'I stopped by the school on my way home,' she confided.

'And?'

'Her form teacher, Mrs Gilbert, confirmed that Laura had missed several days of school since Christmas. And there's worse. This is the third day in a row that she hasn't been to school.'

Dan frowned.

'But why didn't they tell us this earlier? It's ridiculous!' He shoved his hand distractedly through his hair. 'I just don't understand what's going on, Kathleen. She never used to play truant . . . '

'I know. But she's not been herself, has she?' Kathleen reasoned. 'I've been concerned about her for a while. But I couldn't coax her to tell me what was wrong. She's such a dark horse.'

'Don't go blaming yourself.'

'I'm not,' Kathleen snapped.

Dan winced and looked away.

'I just meant that there may be a simple explanation.'

'But this is so out of character for Laura! She's usually so conscientious.'

'Are any of the other girls missing from her class? Could she have gone with them?'

'Mrs Gilbert said it was just Laura — and that she's been withdrawn lately and her work has slipped. Honestly, Dan, she made me feel like the worst parent.' Kathleen sighed.

She set down her cup and it rattled on its saucer as she stood up.

'Where are you going?' Dan asked, rising stiffly to his feet.

'To look for her.'

'But where?'

'I don't know. But I can't just sit here, can I?' She snatched up her car keys, pausing in her flustered state to give her husband a brief hug. 'I have to do something, Dan. Would you mind trying the phone again?'

'Of course not.' He tried to smother his frustration at his own inadequacies.

'You take the mobile and I'll ring you if I hear anything.'

'Likewise, love,' Kathleen promised, heading for the door.

Dan watched her go, then went back into the living-room and sat down by the telephone. Who else could he try?

Driving round the town, Kathleen began to wonder if she was on a fool's errand. Did she really have any chance of finding Laura?

If she was playing truant, and if this really wasn't the first time, then she would probably arrive home at her usual time. Perhaps she ought to go back to the house and wait?

But no, she had to keep looking. Sitting at home, twiddling her thumbs, would be impossible.

She tried to think of favourite places that Laura might go to hide out. Most girls her age were mad on fashion and pop music, but her daughter had never seemed keen on either. She was more interested in reading, animals and athletics. So where did that leave her? Where would Laura go?

'How Did You Find Out?'

After an hour spent checking museums, coffee shops and the park that lay between the house and the school, Kathleen was becoming increasingly anxious.

She drove back along the broad street

that housed the main local amenities. Tapping her fingers impatiently on the steering-wheel, she waited for a car in front of her to reverse into the library carpark.

The library!

She sped forward to the first vacant space, jumped out of the car and hurried up the steps to the main door.

Earnestly searching the vast ground floor of the lending library, she was disappointed to find no sign of her daughter. This was one of Laura's favourite places.

As she walked disconsolately back towards the entrance, she glanced upwards and decided to check the reference section.

It was hushed. Kathleen walked by the main desk, past tables where people sat quietly reading and forward into the body of the building.

A number of tables in the centre were occupied by people working, books spread out around them, but there was no sign of Laura. Just as she was about to turn back, Kathleen noticed some secluded booths at the far end.

She stepped into the next aisle for a better view and drew in a ragged breath of relief. There was her daughter, head bent over her work.

Kathleen composed herself, and walked forward.

'Laura?'

The girl swung round, shock and guilt registering simultaneously on her face.

'Mum! What are you doing here?'

'I think that's my line, don't you?' Kathleen asked, pulling up a chair. 'What's going on, Laura? Why have you been skipping school?'

Laura heaved an enormous sigh and slumped back in her seat, eyes dulled.

'How did you find out?' she whispered hoarsely.

'The school phoned this morning. Your father and I have been worried sick. We've rung round everyone we could think of and I've been out looking for you for ages.'

'I'm sorry. I didn't mean to cause trouble.'

Kathleen felt a deep pang within her. Reaching out, she cupped Laura's cheek in her hand, turning her face towards her.

'Why, Laura? Why can't you talk to me?'

'I . . . ' Laura broke off when someone came to sit in a nearby booth.

'Come on,' Kathleen decided. 'Pack up your things and we'll find somewhere to talk.'

Laura did as she was bid, stuffing books, files and her pencil case into her bag, and followed her mother out of the library. In the car, Kathleen took out her mobile phone.

'I'll just let your dad know you are safe,' she said, dialling the number. 'Dan, I've found her . . . at the library . . . She's fine.

'We're going to have a chat and we'll be home later, OK? Can you arrange for someone to collect the twins? . . . You already have? Oh, that's brilliant. Thanks, love. See you soon.'

Smiling at the relief in her husband's voice, Kathleen turned to Laura, who sat silently beside her.

'How about we get some drinks or ice-cream and go and sit in the park?'

'OK.'

Confession

Before long they were walking side by side towards a secluded bench which nestled in the shade of a tree beside the duck pond.

Kathleen gave Laura a few moments to finish her ice-cream and relax while she tried to collect her own thoughts into some sort of order.

'Are you ready to tell me what's been going on now?' she asked gently.

Laura shrugged.

'I suppose so.'

'What is it, darling? What's been making you so sad?'

'School,' Laura admitted nervously

after a few moments. 'Well, not school, the people at it.'

'Tell me.'

The girl drew her hands up to her mouth as if praying for the right words to reach her lips.

'It started after half-term when a new girl joined the class. She's really horrible, Mum. I stood up for someone in the year below us when Amanda was picking on her and since then she's turned everyone against me.'

'What about your friends?' Kathleen prompted, shocked at what her daughter was saying.

'They're not my friends any more. Not since Amanda came. Everyone is too frightened of her to speak against her.'

She wiped away the tears that had begun to trickle down her cheeks.

'I just can't stand it any more, Mum.'

Her own eyes smarting, Kathleen gathered her daughter in her arms.

'Darling, why didn't you tell us?'

'I didn't want to worry you. I thought

you had enough on your plate — what with Dad's accident and every-thing . . . '

'Oh, Laura! We'd never not have time for you, too. Not if there was something bothering you.'

Laura sniffed and her mum wiped the tears gently from her face with a cotton hankie.

'I know. But it's not only that . . . They said they'd really hurt me if I told anyone.'

'And did they? Hurt you, I mean?'

'They just pushed me around a bit. But this week they locked me in the boiler-room at school. I was there for the whole day, Mum. It was dreadful. I didn't think I'd ever get out, but one of the girls opened the door before she went home. She made me promise not to tell anyone.'

'Poor love.'

Kathleen sat back and stroked her daughter's flushed, tear-stained cheek.

'I knew something was wrong. You've been so withdrawn and unhappy.'

'I'm sorry.'

'It's not your fault. And all this started because you went to help someone else?'

'Yes. And because I didn't like the things they did. And everything I did was wrong, different or stupid.

'I didn't mean to lie to you, but when things got so bad I couldn't face school, I'd go to the library instead and work there. I thought I could handle it. I mean, it's only a few weeks until the end of term. But after they locked me in that room I couldn't go back.'

'You won't have to go back any more, darling, I promise you that.' Kathleen hugged Laura reassuringly close, knowing that Dan would agree. She also knew how upset he would be when he learned what had been going on.

'Everything will be OK now, won't it, Mum?' Laura sniffed.

'Absolutely. Come on, let's go home.'

As they walked back to the car, a new closeness grew between them. Laura turned to Kathleen with a weak smile, the burden visibly lifted from her shoulders.

'Just think, Mum, soon we'll be in Ireland. It'll be perfect!'

A Wrench

The hotel kitchen was filled with the familiar scents of home-baked bread, grilled bacon and freshly-brewed coffee when Stephen arrived. Josie, the kitchen help, was elbow deep in pots and pans, and the dishwasher hummed as it tackled the crockery from guests' breakfasts.

'Busy morning?' he asked his mother as she bustled in with a tray.

'I'll say!' Josie answered for her, her round, kindly face creased with smiles under her cap of auburn hair.

'We had unexpected arrivals last night and we're full to bursting as it is,' Mary Fitzgerald explained. 'Your da is just arranging cycle-hire for the Brooks-Hamiltons. They want to take a trip out to Kate Kearney's Cottage and through the park. Are their packed lunches ready, Josie?'

Josie dried her hands and fetched the picnic food.

'Sure, Mary, shall I take them through for you?' she offered.

'Grand. Thanks, Josie. I couldn't manage without you! Take your break when you're done, now.'

'Are the Brook-whatevers the American family who managed to maroon themselves out on the lough?' Stephen asked. The smell of the bacon had got to him and he made himself a quick sandwich from the left-overs, before Josie returned and told him off.

'Yes, that's the Brooks-Hamiltons. Let's hope their unruly youngsters don't create any more havoc before they go home.'

Stephen grinned at the exasperation on his mother's face.

'Not long now, Mam, and you'll be out of it!'

'And thank the good Lord for that.'

She poured herself a coffee and sat down beside him. 'We've explained our plans to everyone. It's only fair.

'Bridge and Maeve are up there, making the beds right now. I expect they're having a good gossip about it all.'

Stephen knew how much the staff respected and loved his parents. It would be a wrench for them when the hotel changed hands.

'How are things going?' he asked now.

'Grand! The first chap who viewed made an offer. Can you believe it! Of course, it helps that we've had a sudden rush of summer bookings. It's more encouraging when business is booming.

'Your da and I are going to see the solicitor this morning. Will you be around for a while?'

Deciding that his own plans for a day out on the hills could wait, Stephen nodded.

'Sure. I'll hold the fort.'

'Any news of Roisin?' his mother

asked after a few moments.

'No.' Stephen frowned. 'I don't really expect to hear from her, Mam. It's over.'

'Well, I can't say that I'm sorry, son. I was never that keen on her,' Mary admitted frankly. 'Your da and I just want to see you happy — like our Kathleen.'

'I know. But we all have different ways of being happy, Mam.'

'Aren't you the grand philosopher this morning!' Kevin Fitzgerald teased as he joined them. 'Is your mam matchmaking for you?'

'Get away!' Mary protested.

Stephen smiled. That was exactly what his mother would try as soon as the opportunity arose.

'I'm quite capable of organising my own life, thank you. I'm a big boy now.

'And I'm busy at work, too. We have a new student coming in a couple of weeks' time — the last thing we need! You can imagine who'll have the job of baby-sitting.'

'That's because you not only have an expansive knowledge of the territory, but the patience to share it,' his father said warmly.

'Well, if this one is anything like the last, I'll need the patience of a saint, for sure!'

'Where's this one coming from?' his mother asked.

'Canada. But we don't know all the details yet. It's an exchange, so one of us will have the chance to go there.'

'Perhaps it will be you.'

Stephen shook his head.

'I doubt it. Anyway, I'm happy here.'

After a few more minutes of companionable chat, Kevin drained the last of his coffee and rose to his feet.

'Well, come on then, Mary girl, we'd best be off to old McFee's to look over these contracts.'

Smiling, Stephen watched them go. He hoped their dreams would come true.

The telephone rang, snapping him out of his reverie. Stephen went into the office to answer it, pulling the register forward in case it was a booking.

'Waterside Hotel.'

'Stephen!' his sister's voice said in surprise.

'Hi, Kathleen. How are things?'

'Grand. Well, they are now. We had some trouble with Laura, but it's all sorted out, thank goodness.'

Frowning, Stephen twisted the phone cord absent-mindedly through his fingers.

'What kind of trouble?'

'Well, did I mention she'd seemed withdrawn lately?'

'Yes, you'd said. But she was fine at Easter.'

'Exactly,' Kathleen agreed. 'I'd hoped that that was the turning point. But things deteriorated after we returned home and she started playing truant.

'Dan and I were distraught when the school telephoned. It turned out she was being bullied. Dan was livid. He gave the school a real roasting!

'We've taken her out for the last few

weeks and I'm sure she will settle down now.'

'So where will she go to school next year?' Stephen asked, upset that his gentle, sweet-natured niece had been through so much.

Kathleen's laugh tinkled lightly down the wire.

'Ah, well, that's the thing! I really need to talk with Mam or Da. Are they there?'

'No,' Stephen said, puzzled by his sister's change of tack. 'They've gone to see their solicitor to arrange the sale of the hotel. They've found a buyer . . . '

'But they can't have!' Kathleen interrupted. 'Oh, Stephen, you have to stop them!'

'Why? What's the matter? What on earth's going on, Kathleen?' he demanded.

'We want the hotel, Stephen. Dan and I want to take it over and come back to Ireland with the children, to live!'

Too Late?

Stephen felt winded. Wasn't this a bolt from the blue?

'Are you serious?'

'Of course I'm serious! We've thought of little else since Easter. You have to stop them signing anything, please — before it's too late.'

'OK. Calm down. I'll try,' he promised. 'I have McFee's number here so I'll ring straight away. I just hope I'm not too late.' He hesitated.

'You're sure about this. Kathleen?'

'I've never been more sure of anything,' she insisted. 'It'll be a new life for Dan — for us all.

'Oh, Stephen, we've been banking on this. Everyone is so looking forward to moving to Ireland. I could never tell them it's all off.'

★   ★   ★

'Did you have a good time?' Nicola asked, delighted to see Sam as he

95

hopped off the coach at the local cricket ground.

'It was great!' he enthused. 'Especially as we won! Let me get my stuff and I'll tell you about it on the way home.'

Before long, his heavy sports bag tossed over his shoulder, Sam had Nicola's hand in his and they were walking along the road to her house.

'I really missed you.' He smiled, stopping now he was out of sight of his team-mates to kiss her.

'Me, too. But I'm glad you enjoyed yourself.'

'What about you? How did you get on?'

'Fine!' Nicola beamed, anxious to tell him all about her induction day at the veterinary practice. 'All the staff are brilliant. I think I'm going to be really happy there, even if it is just for the holidays.' Her eyes sparkled with joy.

Sam grinned. The enthusiasm in her voice spoke volumes.

'I'm really pleased for you.'

'I'm sure this is right for me, Sam. Even if it does mean years of study and hard work!'

'Rather you than me!'

Tucking her arm through his, Nicola smiled.

'Well, you're settled, too. Are you looking forward to being at the garage full-time?'

'I can't wait. The money may not be much to begin with, but I'll be independent, at last. And in another few months I'll be able to take my driving-test. When I have my licence and more experience under my belt, I'll be able to do so much more at the garage.'

'I Won't Be Coming With You'

They chatted on about their plans until they reached Nicola's house. It was quiet, as her parents were out at work, so they made some sandwiches for lunch and cuddled up on the sofa.

'Have you told your family about the garage?' Nicola asked.

Sam shook his head.

'Not yet. I'd planned to do it this weekend.' He wasn't looking forward to the prospect and suppressed a wave of anxiety.

'I'm so proud of you,' Nicola murmured, snuggling against him. 'I'm sure your parents will be, too.'

As he walked home a short while later, their conversation fresh in his mind, Sam wished he shared Nicola's confidence in his parents' response to his news. He approached the front door, but as he stepped inside, he immediately became aware of an unusual tension in the house.

'What's going on?' he asked.

James was sitting glumly at the top of the stairs.

'We're waiting.'

'What for?' Sam demanded.

'We're not allowed to say,' Luke put in, stepping out of the twins' bedroom and poking James to silence.

His brothers' cryptic responses frustrated Sam even further and he went in search of his parents.

He found them in the living-room, watching TV.

'Sam!' his mother exclaimed, rising to hug him. 'It's good to have you home. Have you eaten?'

'I had something at Nic's.' He looked from one parent to the other. 'Is something the matter?'

'Not exactly, son. It's just . . . ' his father began. He was silenced by the sudden ring of the telephone.

His mother dashed to answer it, and Sam stood in amazement as the twins clattered down the stairs and Laura appeared from the kitchen. They had all gone potty in his absence!

'Mam? Hello . . . No, no . . . I'm sure it was a surprise! I was going to ring you — but . . . well . . . we just never imagined things would begin to move so soon!'

Sam glanced across at Laura, but his sister, who he noticed was looking much more animated than when he'd left, only smiled in return.

'So what do you and Da think?' Kathleen continued, reaching out a hand to clasp Dan's. 'Really! We can! Marvellous! Look, Mam, I'll ring you back in a few moments. The eyes and ears of the world are upon me, desperate to hear the news. Five minutes, Mam. Promise.'

She put the phone down and turned to face her family, grinning from ear to ear.

'Is it yes?' Laura asked.

'It's a great big yes!'

His parents hugged and the twins and Laura began whooping and dancing around the room. Sam's confusion increased momentarily before it instantly became clear.

'You're going to Ireland, aren't you?'

The whole family stopped in its tracks. His father nodded.

'Yes, son. It all came about rather suddenly while you were away, although your mother and I have been talking about it for some time.'

'I see.'

'I know it's a shock, Sam.' His mother smiled weakly, searching his expression for a reaction. 'How do you feel about it?'

'I'm happy for you if that's what you want. I know things have been difficult since Dad's accident.' He was surprised how calm he felt now the moment had arrived.

His father sat back down.

'But?' Dan prompted softly.

'But I have plans of my own.

'Before I left for the cricket trip, I was offered a permanent position at the garage — full training and a guaranteed job at the end of it.'

His mother raised one hand to her mouth; Sam had certainly taken the wind from her sails. But more was to come.

Sam took a deep breath as he held his mother's gaze.

'I've accepted the offer. I won't be coming with you.'

New Beginnings

Kathleen sat back, enjoying the feel of the sun on her face, the heat of the early August day offset by the breeze off the sea. Beneath her the engines of the ferry hummed, the deck vibrating. They had been at sea for a couple of hours now, the Welsh coast and mainland Britain slipping out of sight behind them as they set out on this new adventure.

'I still can't quite believe we're really on our way,' she commented as Dan returned with cold drinks.

'It's certainly been a hectic few weeks,' he allowed with a smile, easing himself uncomfortably on to the seat beside her. 'I never expected things would fall into place so smoothly. Fancy the very first family falling in love with the house! It could have taken weeks, months!'

The sale had been agreed and contracts exchanged, although the new owners would not be moving in for some weeks yet. Kathleen still felt quite dizzy at the speed with which everything had happened once the decision had been made. There had been so much to do, so much to arrange!

The removals lorry would be following them to Ireland the next day. And there was still so much to organise once they arrived in Killarney. Schools for the children, banks, doctors, all manner of things, not to mention getting to grips with the running of the hotel!

'It suddenly seems so daunting!' she said now, turning to face Dan, seeing the contentment and anticipation on his handsome face.

'We'll manage, and your parents will be on hand to guide us through the sticky bits,' he reassured.

Kathleen envied his equanimity. Did he feel none of the nervous misgivings that nagged at her? He had never wavered in his belief. Nor had the children. Laura was happier than ever, more confident, more secure, tanned and at ease, Kathleen admitted, watching her now as she leaned on the rail, watching the seabirds that swirled and dipped beside the ship. The twins were bundles of barely restrained excitement! They were occupied now with organised games elsewhere on the deck, running off their energy and relieving the boredom of the long ferry crossing.

Which just left Sam, Kathleen acknowledged, a pang of loss bringing a hollow feeling to her stomach. She sighed, recalling the moment of parting, how she'd held back her own tears as her son, now a young man, had been left behind.

'It'll be all right,' Dan said now, reaching out for her hand, sensing her disquiet.

'Of course.' She managed a bright smile, despite her concerns. 'I just worry about splitting the family. I didn't want this to happen.'

'I know, love. But we have to accept that Sam has grown up. He's behaved with great maturity about it all and he has already settled down well at work.'

Kathleen nodded, unable to deny that her son's sudden independence had impressed her. 'I do feel better knowing that he's living in his boss's flat above the garage.'

'Brian and Avril are good family people,' Dan agreed. 'They'll take care of Sam. Brian was telling me that our boy is a natural and has a very good career ahead of him. I know it's hard, seeing the first one fly the nest, but it would have been wrong to stand in his way.'

'And he has Nicola. She's such a level-headed girl who'll go far herself. Not to mention all his friends and their families,' Kathleen added with a tremulous smile.

'Exactly.' Dan gave her hand another squeeze, sounding relieved. 'Anyway, we're not so far away. He'll be visiting, and if things don't work out as he'd hoped, he can always join us.'

Kathleen wished that all the reassurances and knowledge that Sam was cared for and happy would banish the last of the doubts she harboured about whether they had done the right thing. There had been hours, days, of talking. Sam had been determined, so grown up and together about them leaving him. Laura had been shocked and sad at first, but the prospect of Ireland had soon overtaken any feelings she may have had about her elder brother staying behind. The twins barely seemed to have noticed in their excitement.

Finishing his drink, Dan eased his aching body, looking forward to journey's end. He found the travelling very wearing. He hoped he had allayed some of Kathleen's fears — hoped that his own anxieties had been well hidden and not given her any more cause for concern.

Leaving Sam behind had been much more of a wrench than he had admitted to anyone. Was he just trying to convince himself the boy was old enough to cope with his new independence and life away from the family?

Dan worried. Was he so determined to reach for this dream he'd not properly considered the effects it would have on them all? No matter how much he told himself they were doing the right thing, flickers of doubt remained. Among them the doubt about his own capabilities of managing this new life.

'I can see land!' Laura announced, bouncing back to join them. 'Do come and look!'

'We ought to get the boys,' Kathleen said. 'They won't want to miss this.'

'I'll go!'

Laura bounded away, blonde plait bobbing down her back, and Dan laughed.

'It's good to see her so happy and full of life again.'

'Yes, it is,' Kathleen agreed, watching her daughter disappear to find her brothers. 'We are doing the right thing, aren't we, Dan?'

Slipping his arm around her shoulders, he drew her close, making her feel loved and protected and cherished. 'It's a second chance for us, love, a new life.'

They watched as the Tusker Rock Lighthouse hove into view, the craggy coastline of Ireland, their new home, coming closer and closer. The children rushed to join them, chattering excitedly as the ferry chugged towards the harbour.

Hugging Dan back, Kathleen looked up at him, her eyes brimming with emotion. He was right, this was a new chance for them, a whole new beginning. Gathering the three children towards them, they shared a special smile, one that held hope and love and nervous excitement as they made their pact.

'Whatever the future holds, we'll face it together.'

4

Old Friends

'Kathleen! I can't believe you're really here! It's grand having you home again!'

Teresa Harrington burst into the hotel kitchen like a whirlwind.

Laughing, Kathleen exchanged an enthusiastic hug with her old friend, then stepped back.

'You look fantastic. Barely a day older!'

'Get away with you,' Teresa protested, smoothing down some tousled wisps of dark hair, her eyes shining. 'How can you still be as slender as a reed after four children?'

The intervening years slipped away amidst their easy banter; they were teenagers again.

'Have you time for a coffee? Mam

109

and Dad have taken the children up to the new bungalow, so we'll have the place to ourselves for a while.'

'Grand. I'll just bring your order in first.'

While fresh coffee was percolating, Kathleen began to put away the milk and Teresa's lovely home-made dairy products, remembering to check them off against the delivery note.

Teresa's parents, Joe and Patsy O'Connor, had run the small farm for as long as Kathleen could remember. Before retiring, they had diversified and now specialised in home-made cheese, yoghurts, ice-cream and butter. Teresa's family had supplied local businesses, including the hotel, for a few years now and the regular contact between the families meant Kathleen and Teresa had kept up to date with each other's news, despite rarely seeing each other.

'How are you enjoying being your own boss, Teresa?' Kathleen asked once they were seated with their coffee.

'Honestly, Kathleen, we're that busy, we've had to take on more staff, especially now we have the internet orders, too,' Teresa explained. 'It's funny, I never imagined I'd end up taking over when Ma and Pa sloped off into the sunset, but I really enjoy it now.'

'I hope to be saying the same thing, shortly.'

Teresa smiled at her friend and helped herself to a thickly-buttered soda scone.

'I was amazed when your mam told me you were coming home. Delighted, of course, but it was the last thing I thought you would do.'

'Me, too! But when I knew the old place was to be sold — and once Dan had sown the seed of the idea — I realised how much it meant to me. And he was dead keen to give it a go! I have to give it a chance, Teresa. Dan's determined to make a new life here.'

'We were sorry to hear about his accident, Kathleen.' Teresa's face took on a sombre aspect. 'How's he doing now?'

'Not bad, thanks. He keeps to himself a lot. I know he's often uncomfortable, but his determination to make this work is carrying him through.

'It's been hectic right enough, what with selling the house, buying this place and trying to get the children into schools.'

'I can imagine. Are you going to see Sister Phil about Laura?'

'This afternoon.' Kathleen nodded. She and Teresa both smiled at the thought of their old form teacher, now headmistress.

'My Fiona will be in the same class. If you have time, why not bring Laura up this afternoon when you've finished? They can start getting to know each other properly.'

Kathleen nodded.

'That's a grand idea! Laura had a rough time at her old school. It would be good for her to make friends with Fiona before term starts. Thanks,

Teresa, we'll call in later on.'

'I'll look forward to it. We can have another chinwag.' Her old friend grinned, rising to her feet. 'Thanks for the coffee. I'd best finish my deliveries or they'll be sending out a search party for me!'

★   ★   ★

'Do you remember Teresa?' Kathleen asked Laura a little later. They had just drawn up at the Harringtons' farm and Laura was standing rather awkwardly at the door of the warm, welcoming but chaotic farmhouse kitchen.

'I think so,' Laura murmured nervously.

'Sure, the poor girl was only knee high to a grasshopper the last time we met.' Teresa laughed. 'You've grown into a beautiful young lady, Laura.'

Laura blushed at the compliment, but smiled back, liking her mother's old friend at once.

'Thank you.'

'Come away in, both of you.'

A ginger cat was sitting on the kitchen chair, and Laura paused to stroke it. It purred contentedly, while she listened to the grown-ups chatting.

'The place looks grand,' Kathleen told her friend. Teresa set the kettle on the range to boil.

'We've still a lot of improvements to make, but you should see the new milking machinery — state of the art, or what! Ma and Pa would be amazed if they could see it.'

'I'm sure they'll be very proud of you.'

Kathleen touched her friend's arm gently, aware how much Teresa was missing her parents. Mr and Mrs O'Connor had recently decided to see out their retirement in Malaga and Teresa, who'd always been close to her mum, was finding the long-distance relationship hard to adapt to.

'How is Jack liking it here?'

Teresa grinned.

'As long as he doesn't have to get

involved with the farming side of things he's fine! He loves working with the horses and not having to travel all the time.

'It's going well. He's making a good name for himself, producing competition animals. And he's bringing on a couple of star pupils.'

'Fantastic, Teresa!' Kathleen beamed.

Full Circle

It was strange, she thought, how in some ways their lives had run parallel. And now they both had come full circle.

For years Teresa had travelled around with her husband, Jack, a well-known showjumper. He had represented Ireland at the last Olympics, before retiring from competition at the height of his success.

'He's surprised me,' Teresa admitted. 'I was worried he wouldn't settle here.'

Kathleen stared out of the window at

the sweeping views of the hills.

'You know, I'd forgotten how beautiful it is here.'

'We've had some grand times out on those hills, haven't we?'

'The best.'

Smiling, Teresa turned to Laura.

'Your ma and I have quite a history!' she began, only to pause as footsteps sounded in the yard outside and the door burst open. A tall, slender girl with rich brown hair, freckled cheeks and sparkling eyes entered.

'Oh, Ma! You should have called me . . . I wanted to be here when you came!' she cried in disappointment. 'Hi, Mrs Jackson, I've heard so much about you. Ma talks about you all the time.'

'Does she now?' Kathleen laughed. 'I hardly dare imagine! It's lovely to see you, Fiona . . . and, please, call me Kathleen.' Aware of her daughter's shyness, she drew her forward.

'This is Laura. Say hello, love.'

'Laura, it's brilliant that you're here! Ma, can I take Laura to look around?'

116

'Yes, of course.' Teresa grinned. 'Kathleen and I will catch up on the gossip over our tea.'

Laura didn't have time to be shy. Fiona's bubbly personality simply overwhelmed her, sweeping away any uncertainty. She chattered constantly and was so full of energy that before they had even left the house Laura felt quite exhausted.

'I'll show you round the farm first, then the stables.' Fiona breezed through the kitchen and pulled on a seemingly random pair of wellingtons from the stacks that lay higgledy-piggledy in the back porch.

'Help yourself.' She gestured at the odd assortment. 'Your trainers will be ruined otherwise.'

Besotted

Struggling to keep up, Laura found a pair of boots that fitted and trailed in her new friend's wake. They visited the parlour, where the gentle-eyed cows waited patiently for milking, shaded from the hot summer sun.

Then Fiona showed her the rows and rows of different cheeses and the freezers full of ice-creams and yoghurts.

'We've some cool new flavours.' Fiona grinned. 'Coconut and lime is my favourite. You'll have to try some.'

'That sounds lovely,' Laura said shyly.

Fiona took Laura's arm and steered her across the yard and down a farm track.

'Let's see the stables now. Do you ride, Laura?'

'No, but I've always wanted to. I love animals, especially dogs and horses.'

'Me, too!' Fiona grinned her approval. 'We have masses here. Ma is always bringing home waifs and strays. Me da gets quite demented about it!'

'Your mum said he works with horses?'

'He was a showjumper. We used to go all over — to shows and stuff, you know. He rode for Ireland! He brings on horses and riders now,' Fiona chattered on. 'We have some grand riding round here. You'll love it, Laura. There's so much we can explore together.'

'I think I'd probably need some riding lessons,' she ventured shyly.

'I'll teach you. Don't worry.'

They wandered round the stables and paddocks, Fiona telling her about the horses, including her own beloved iron-grey gelding, Frosty. Laura loved it all; the silken coats and velvety noses, the kindly brown eyes, and warm, horsey smells.

'Me da's out looking at some young stock,' Fiona explained. 'You'll have to come up one morning and watch when they're schooling. Declan's a grand rider.'

'I'd love to.' Laura imagined the graceful horses taking the practice jumps in the sand school with ease.

'Come on! I must show you the puppies.' Fiona led the way back to the farmhouse at a run.

'Nell is me da's Labrador. She had her litter about four weeks ago.' She opened a door into a warm annexe off the kitchen and gently brought out into the sunshine the sweetest puppies Laura had ever seen.

'Aren't they adorable?'

Sinking to her knees, Laura laughed as the tiny chocolate coloured bundles scrambled to see over the sides of the container, while their mother looked on unperturbed. Soon Laura was besotted.

'Oh, Fiona, they're beautiful!'

'There are still a couple without homes to go to. We're going to keep one. Why don't you ask your ma if you can have one, too?'

'If only I could,' Laura whispered fervently, stroking the warm, wriggling bodies. 'If only I could.'

The door opened, disturbing her dreams.

'I might have known you'd be here.' Teresa smiled. 'Come on, girls, Kathleen is waiting.'

Reluctantly, Laura returned to the kitchen.

'I had a brilliant time,' she told her mother, her eyes shining with excitement.

'I'm glad you and Fiona are making friends. But we must fly or we'll be late for the guests' suppers!'

Second Thoughts

'Are you sure you'll manage all right on your own?' Kathleen asked Dan, coming into the office after the breakfast rush and setting a cup of coffee down on the desk.

'Of course. Thanks for the coffee.'

'Are you all right?'

Dan forced a tight smile in response to her concern.

'I'm fine, I just haven't recovered properly from the journey yet.

'You know, it's a relief your parents never did sit-down lunches. It looks like we'll be pressed enough with breakfasts and evening meals.'

'I know. They've always said it was only in these few hours in the middle of the day that they could catch up on other work. At least Josie has appointed herself in charge of packed lunches.'

'She's been a godsend,' Dan agreed. 'All the staff have. They seem to have accepted us taking over.'

'I think they're just pleased to be keeping their jobs. At least it's all in the family.'

Sipping his coffee, he watched as Kathleen searched for her car keys and cheque book.

'Is there anything you need while we're out?' she asked after a moment.

'No, thanks.'

'I'm just going to get Laura's uniform sorted out, and I'm taking the boys with me; they need new shoes. We won't be long.'

'Take your time.'

'Dan . . . ?'

He glanced up to find she had paused at the door, a frown on her face.

'Yes?'

'Never mind.' She shook her head. 'Oh, by the way, Stephen said he might pop in.'

Alone at last, Dan rubbed at the pain in his back, and heaved an exhausted sigh. The enormity of the task they were taking on had only hit him since he'd been to the bank the day before, and he had still not properly discussed their financial situation with Kathleen. He didn't for a moment believe that Kevin and Mary had hidden anything from them. And the condition of the hotel had never been a secret.

But in the excitement of the move, perhaps he had allowed his heart to rule his head. He had failed to realise just how much work and money it would take to set things right. That had been brought home to him all too forcefully during his meeting with the bank manager.

It was already mid-summer and, although they were busy, they were by no means full. Autumn bookings were down. Dan had no idea if it was a general trend or just them.

He shifted uncomfortably in the chair. On top of that, his unwillingness to admit how much his injuries had been bothering him complicated his ability to communicate. The extra activity had caused more problems than he had imagined and he wondered how long he could go on hiding his discomfort from his wife.

It wasn't fair, after all. Kathleen was as busy as he was. She'd taken on more than her share of the work, and she was seeing to the preparations for Laura, Luke and James starting school.

Despite all that, she seemed relaxed and content — delighted to have returned to Ireland. How long would it last, he asked himself?

Laura, though, had blossomed since they had arrived in Killarney. No doubt her friendship with Fiona Harrington would help her adjust.

Luke spent as much time as he could with his Uncle Stephen and James had formed a special bond with his grandfather. Already he was beginning to emerge from his twin's shadow.

As for Sam . . . ? Dan had spoken to him several times on the phone and had been pleased to find him cheerful and content.

He sighed and drained the last of the coffee. Perhaps he was the only one having second thoughts.

The ringing of the telephone interrupted his reverie.

'Waterside Hotel. Dan Jackson speaking.'

'Hello, Mr Jackson. This is Maureen Delaney.'

'Good morning, Mrs Delaney.' He recognised the crisp, starchy tones that characterised the headmistress of the school the twins would attend.

'I'm pleased to tell you that Luke sailed through the entrance exam. He's a very bright boy and we are pleased to offer him a place when school restarts in September.'

'Thank you. That's excellent news. And James?'

'Yes . . . James.' There was a pause, and Dan's heart sank. 'He did not do so well. I'm sure that's no surprise to you, given his previous school record. I'm afraid James didn't pass the exam, Mr Jackson.'

Dan sighed.

'Can he retake the tests, Mrs Delaney?'

'I would be reluctant to ask James to try again. He found it very stressful, as I'm sure you know. I really don't think this is the place for him, Mr Jackson.'

'I see.' Agitated, he ran his fingers through the springy thickness of his hair. 'I'll have to discuss things with my wife when she comes back.'

'I understand. If you could confirm Luke's place as soon as possible, I'd be most grateful.'

'Of course,' Dan muttered. 'Thank you, Mrs Delaney.'

He hung up the phone with more force than he'd intended.

'Irritating woman!'

All of a sudden he felt the need of

some air and wandered out into the hotel courtyard where Stephen was tending the hanging baskets.

Some Good Advice

'Are you all right, Dan? You look a bit cheesed off. Is there a problem?'

'No more than usual.' Dan shrugged. 'That was Mrs Delaney at the boys' school. Apparently Luke has been accepted but not James.'

'I see.'

Dan dropped wearily on to a garden bench. Stephen frowned and sat down beside him.

'Getting the boys sorted out is proving a lot harder than it was for Laura. I don't know how I'm going to break this latest news to Kathleen.'

'Perhaps it would be a good idea if they were split up,' Stephen ventured after a moment.

'What do you mean?' Dan asked. 'You think we should send them to different schools from the outset?'

'They both have different skills, different interests. Don't take this the wrong way, Dan, but it must be hard for James, always being compared to Luke and feeling that he never measures up.'

'I hadn't thought of it like that.' Dan paused for a moment, remembering the way Luke teased his twin for being slow on the uptake. 'I wonder if it would work.

'Kathleen had her heart set on them going to this school.'

Stephen shrugged.

'It has an excellent record academically, but there are plenty of other good schools locally, ones that better suit children like James. They offer more vocational and practical opportunities. James is a doer, Dan, not a thinker.'

'Maybe,' Dan agreed, warming to the idea. 'I'll discuss it with Kath.'

'Have her call Liam Flanagan. He's an old pal of hers and he's head of a small school on the outskirts of town. It has a great reputation.'

'Thanks, Stephen, I'll do that.

'The others will be back for lunch soon. Will you stay and eat with us?'

'I was hoping you'd ask!' The younger man grinned. 'I need fortifying.'

Dan temporarily set his worries aside and sat back with a smile.

'How so?'

'You know we have a student coming on placement to the National Park for a year?'

'From Canada. You said.' Dan smiled, remembering Stephen's accounts of past experiences. 'Ach, you'll be a dab hand at supervising now — after that last lad you had.'

'That's not funny!' Stephen lamented. 'Anyway, the flight is due in later this afternoon and I've drawn the short straw — I'm the chauffeur.'

First Impressions

The view of Ireland's rugged west coast was largely obscured by cloud as the plane neared the end of its journey and prepared to land at Shannon Airport.

It had been a long flight and Annie felt tired and stiff. The manner of her departure from home had left her feeling grumpy and preoccupied. All she wanted now was to complete the trip to Killarney with as little delay and stress as possible.

By the time she had passed through all the security checks and been reunited with her baggage, the tension headache that had nagged at her for several hours was beating a calypso beneath her scalp. Feeling nauseous, she pushed her trolley ahead of her and scanned the line of waiting people, searching for the one expecting her.

She spotted a man holding a card which read *Killarney National Park — Webster*. Annie applied a polite smile and walked forward.

The man had not yet noticed her. She guessed he was around thirty, tall and lean, with an attractive face and a thatch of thick dark hair. He looked round as she approached, his eyes an intense blue.

Their gazes locked and held for several tense, silent seconds.

'I think you are waiting for me,' she announced frostily. Her voice was more clipped than she had intended.

One neat, dark eyebrow rose as he continued to look at her. He shook his head.

'Are you Annie Webster?'

'I am. Is there a problem?'

'No. Of course not. Welcome to Ireland.'

'Thank you.'

Folding his sign into his pocket, Stephen moved to take charge of the trolley.

'Would you care to freshen up, or have a drink before we leave?'

'No, thank you. I'd sooner we made tracks if that's all right,' she responded. She refused to relinquish her hold on the trolley and set off abruptly towards the exit.

Prickly, Stephen thought. She wasn't

at all what he had been expecting. Mid to late-twenties, she was a few years older than their usual students. And even tired and ruffled from her flight, there was no denying that Annie was an attractive woman.

He watched her as she walked ahead of him. Despite her jeans and loose-fitting shirt, she cut a shapely figure.

'The Land-Rover is just over here,' he announced, guiding her through the curtain of rain to the waiting vehicle.

'I'm sorry; it's the best I could do.'

'It's fine.'

'I meant the weather.'

His humour went unrewarded. She allowed him to stow her bags in the back, then climbed inside to keep dry while he returned the trolley.

'Have you been to Ireland before?' he asked, shaking off the rain and sliding behind the wheel.

'No.'

As he drove away from the airport and headed home towards County Kerry, Stephen glanced across at her.

She was a strange one. Still and silent beside him, she'd barely said a word since he'd picked her up. Stephen found his passenger's uncommunicative mood at odds with his easy-going nature.

If first impressions were anything to go by, having Annie Webster around for the next year would not be plain sailing.

Disappointment

'Has Laura mentioned puppies to you?' Kathleen asked. She and Dan were enjoying a rare mid-morning break together in the kitchen.

Dan smiled. He knew where this was heading.

'Only a few hundred times.'

'She's getting on so well with Fiona.'

'I know, and I'm glad. It'll help her settle in when she starts school.'

Kathleen nodded, tracing an idle pattern on the table top with her fingers.

'What do you think about it?'

'About what?' Dan asked. He was

preoccupied with the autumn bookings and James's schooling.

'Laura having a puppy.'

'I've no objection in principle. I love animals.' Dan sighed. 'But I don't see how we can cope with a puppy on top of everything else right now.'

'It's just that Laura's had such a difficult time. I think it would be good for her.'

'Perhaps.' Dan frowned. 'But who would look after it when she's at school?

'Look, let's not try to run before we can walk, Kath.'

Knowing Dan was right didn't ease Kathleen's underlying disappointment for Laura.

'Can we at least give it some thought?' she persisted. 'Teresa says the puppies won't be ready for another few weeks. And she's offered to help out any time, if Laura was allowed to have one.'

'We'll see. There are more pressing things to worry about at the moment — James, for instance.'

Kathleen watched as Dan drained his

134

coffee. He had been so preoccupied this last week or so and was daft enough to think she hadn't noticed. A distance seemed to have opened up between them and she was finding it difficult to pin him down to a discussion.

'I've been thinking over what Stephen said,' she admitted. 'How do you feel about it?'

'Well, it makes sense. It's not fair to hold Luke back when he has the chance of a place at such a good school. And he seems keen to go. But, even if they would have accepted him, James would have hated it there. Perhaps a smaller, vocationally oriented school is what he needs.'

Kathleen nodded, glancing up with a smile as her parents came into the kitchen.

A Blast From The Past

'We were just talking about James,' she said as they joined them at the table.

'I have to say, Kathleen, I think

Stephen is right,' Kevin volunteered.

'I agree. It would give James a chance to develop his own interests,' Mary ventured. 'And it's just as good a school.'

Kathleen exchanged a glance with Dan.

'So we'll go and see them then?' she asked.

'Stephen suggested you phone the head first.' Dan fished in his pocket for the piece of paper with the name his brother-in-law had given him. 'Here we are. A man called Liam Flanagan.'

'Good grief!' Kathleen exclaimed. 'There's a blast from the past!' She swallowed quickly, attempting to regain her composure. 'Is he really the head teacher?'

'He is indeed!' Her father laughed.

'Stephen said you knew him?' Dan asked.

'Yes. I did. Years ago.' Kathleen smiled, aware of the heat staining her cheeks pink.

'Quite sweet on him, you were!' Mary teased.

'Oh, Mam, get away!' Kathleen's

136

blush deepened and she looked away.

'You were, too,' Kevin chipped in. 'He was a grand lad; good-looking and mad keen on rugby.'

Dan sat back, unsure why he felt so disconcerted.

In nearly twenty years of marriage, Kathleen had never mentioned this man. Yet he had obviously meant something to her.

As the teasing continued he fell silent, very much aware that he was suddenly an outsider.

★   ★   ★

'I'm sorry, Sam. I'm going to have to cancel tonight,' Nicola apologised.

'But why?' he demanded. 'I thought you were looking forward to seeing this film.'

'I was. I am. But something has come up.'

'What?'

'Well, I have the chance of observing at a major operation,' she explained excitedly. 'It's complicated, so it's likely to take ages and it's not the type of procedure that crops up every day. This is really important, Sam.'

And I'm not, he thought sulkily, as she rang off. She hadn't even wanted to make arrangements for the weekend. Disgruntled, he wandered round the small, stark bedsit, wondering what to do with himself.

He had so looked forward to embracing his independence, not only working full-time and training as a mechanic, but also spending more time with Nicola. He took a can of cola and leftover sandwich from the fridge, and plonked himself down on the shabby sofa. Nothing had turned out as he had expected.

Working at the garage on Saturdays and in school holidays was quite different from being the junior apprentice. The lure of the racing cars had been strong, but he'd not even been allowed to watch yet, let alone help in the pits.

As for Nicola, this wasn't the first time she'd let him down over the past few weeks. The veterinary practice was all she could talk about.

Frowning, Sam rose to his feet and tossed the remains of the sandwich into the bin. Rather than setting him free, his decision to stay in England had unsettled him more than he'd realised. It was far harder being independent than he had anticipated.

It was Sunday before he saw Nicola again. They finally made it to the cinema, but as they stood in the queue outside, warmed by the August sun, he felt awkward.

'What's wrong?' Nicola asked, linking her arm through his.

'I don't know.' He shrugged, unwilling to admit his misgivings. 'I suppose I'm missing my family more than I expected.'

'Well, you were bound to,' she pointed out.

Sam bit his tongue to avoid snapping at her. He knew she wasn't being deliberately condescending. It was his own mood that was to blame for his irritability. As if sensing his disquiet, Nicola looked up at him.

'Are you regretting your decision? Do you wish you had gone to Ireland, after all?'

'No,' he said forcefully as they edged forwards in the queue. 'Of course not. What would I do there?'

Nicola frowned thoughtfully.

'It's early days, Sam. Things will settle down.'

Wanting to be reassured, and to please her, he managed a smile.

'You're probably right.'

They finally entered the cinema and bought popcorn and drinks before taking their seats.

'How about you?' he asked, trying to sound interested. 'What was the operation like?'

Nicola's eyes sparkled as she turned to face him.

'It was great, even better than I expected. Honestly, Sam, I'm learning so much. If I stick in there may even be a job for me helping with in-patients at the weekends.'

Sam took a sip of his drink. He was glad for Nicola. She was doing what she wanted to do and she was happy. He felt a chasm grow between them. She was moving on and away; he was standing still.

Yearning

It was still early when he arrived back at the flat after walking Nicola home. As he let himself in, the phone began to ring and he rushed to answer it.

'Hello?'

'Sam! How are you?'

The sound of his mother's voice brought a lump to his throat.

'I'm fine,' he lied, feigning cheeriness. 'How are things going there?'

'Grand, but hectic. There's been so much to sort out.'

He could hear the smile in her voice,

picture her face in his mind.

'How's Dad?'

'Not too bad, love. He's been working hard and I think he's a bit sore, but it's nothing to worry about,' she reassured him, and proceeded to fill him in on what they were doing.

He listened to all the news of the family; the updates on his grandparents' retirement bungalow and the arrival of some feisty woman from Canada who was giving his Uncle Stephen a hard time. Suddenly he was filled with a terrible yearning to be there.

'We love you, Sam. Take care of yourself.'

'Love you, too, Mum,' he said tightly.

He waited until his mother disconnected the call before he could bring himself to hang up the phone. He knew she had no idea how sad and lonely he was. Foolish pride had driven him to hide his despair. Despite his age, he longed for a cuddle.

A hollow ache settled inside him as he went to bed. Clearly, he wasn't as grown up as he had thought he was. But what was he going to do about it?

5

An Appointment To Keep

'We've had a swell time, Ms Jackson.' Buzz Goldman III slapped the counter heartily. 'Mrs Goldman and I will sure be recommending y'all here at Waterside.'

Kathleen smiled and handed over the receipt.

'Thank you, Mr Goldman. I hope you'll visit us again.'

'You can count on it!' The bluff Texan grinned, wedging his credit card back inside an over-stuffed wallet.

'Have a safe journey,' she called as he made his way down the front steps to the hire car, where his equally amiable wife awaited him.

Kathleen waved, resisting the urge to look at her watch. She was conscious that the day was already getting away from her and if they didn't hurry, she and Dan would be late for their appointment to look over the school for James.

She rushed upstairs. At least the staff would hold the fort while they were out. Kathleen hastily washed and changed. Her mind was already brimful of worries. Dan had been so preoccupied over the last day or two, she still hadn't managed to talk to him about Sam.

She knew he had tried to hide it, but their eldest son had sounded so miserable on the telephone. Kathleen was beginning to wonder whether they had done the right thing in allowing him to remain behind in England.

But she didn't have time to dwell on Sam now, she reminded herself. Frowning, she slipped her feet into a pair of smart shoes. If she didn't find Dan soon, they would be seriously late for their meeting with Liam.

Kathleen's frown deepened. That was another thing. She wasn't at all sure it was a good idea to send James to a school where her old flame was head teacher. But Dan had taken Stephen's advice to heart; he was convinced this was the right place for their troublesome twin. So for the moment she'd have to be content to keep her own counsel.

Anxious, Kathleen took a final look in the mirror, brushed aside a wayward dot of mascara, then went in search of her husband.

* * *

Dan winced and steadied himself with his walking-stick. He took a few deep breaths to try to control the jolt of pain that had seared through his back and hip. He knew he had been foolish — his days of climbing ladders were over. But . . .

'Dan? Where are you?'

Kathleen's voice startled him and he glanced guiltily towards the door.

'I'm just coming,' he called, awkwardly moving the ladder out of the way.

'What on earth do you think you're doing?' his wife demanded angrily as she stepped into the room. 'For goodness' sake, Dan!'

'It's all right . . . I . . . '

'No, it isn't all right!' Kathleen interrupted, anger glittering in her clear blue eyes.

A fresh twinge gripped him as he turned to face her, cross at being found out, unsettled by her lack of faith in him.

'Look, there's nothing to fuss about. I was just changing a light bulb.'

'You promised you wouldn't do things like this. What if you had hurt yourself?'

'I'm fine,' he lied. 'Besides, we can't afford to pay a handyman.'

'But . . . '

It was his turn to interrupt.

'Let's not argue about this now, Kathleen. We'll be late for the school at this rate.'

As if it was her fault!

A tense silence filled the car as she drove through the town. Dan's face had that pinched, grey look he was unable to hide when in pain.

Kathleen shook her head. As if she didn't have enough to worry about. The last thing she needed was Dan landing himself back in hospital. Perhaps, she thought, she would feel better once this appointment with Liam was out of the way.

As they waited in the reception area at the small school on the outskirts of town, Kathleen felt her own nervous tension hang in the air between her and Dan. He was quiet and preoccupied, sitting stiffly on the hard-backed chair.

'Are you OK?' she asked, concern softening her voice.

He smiled and reached out to squeeze her hand.

'I'll be fine.'

A Chance To Flourish

She was prevented from speaking again as the door to the head teacher's office

148

opened and a tall, dark-haired man came out to greet them. As he smiled and walked towards them, Kathleen's hand instinctively tightened on Dan's, an uncomfortable knot forming in her stomach.

'Kathleen! It's good to see you again. You're looking great.' Liam smiled, reaching out to shake her hand.

Hesitantly, Kathleen shook it. Her gaze flicked to his face and skittered away again.

'Hello, Liam,' she replied. She slipped her hand through Dan's arm and drew him close.

'This is Dan, my husband.'

'Grand to meet you.' Liam grinned and took Dan's hand. 'Come in, won't you?'

'Thanks.' Dan smiled, and with his hand at the small of Kathleen's back, he ushered her ahead of him. 'And thank you also, Liam, for taking the time to see us before term starts.'

'Oh, sure, it's nothing. Call it a favour to an old friend.'

Dan's limp seemed more pronounced as they crossed Liam's spacious office and he eased himself gingerly on to the chair by the desk. Kathleen sat beside her husband, allowing him to make small talk with Liam for a few moments. Dan described the reasons behind the family's move to Ireland before James himself was mentioned.

Kathleen tuned out the men's voices and drifted back twenty years. Her family still believed her parting from Liam had been an amicable one. She had never told anyone what had happened between them — not Dan, not even Teresa, with whom she had shared all her girlhood secrets.

She supposed the spat between them and what had followed had been such a shock that she had kept it to herself. She had left Ireland shortly after, for England and her nursing position. They hadn't seen each other since.

She had been so nervous about coming here. But there was Liam behaving as if all that had happened was long forgotten.

'I've been over James's reports and the letter from his old school,' Liam was saying now, and Kathleen forced herself to concentrate. 'From that, and all you told me on the phone, Dan, I feel sure we can help him here.'

'Kathleen and I discussed the idea of splitting Luke and James. We do have some reservations about it, but everyone seems to think it may be a good idea.'

Liam nodded.

'I agree. One of the benefits of the education system here, as you are coming to realise, is that we can offer more to those young people who are better suited to a vocational future rather than an academic one. We have an excellent programme of learning in this school — a good academic grounding, naturally, but strong vocational and sporting aspects, also.

'I think James could flourish here.'

They spent some time looking round the school, taking things slowly to accommodate Dan's gait. They became more confident by the moment that they had at last found the right niche for James.

A Bit Of Communication

Back in Liam's office, over coffee, they went over all the paperwork and came to an agreement. Kathleen felt relieved. Not only had they solved James's situation, but meeting Liam again had not been the ordeal she had feared.

'So, it's four children you have altogether?' Liam asked politely, sitting back in his chair with a smile.

'That's right. Laura, our daughter, is fourteen. She and the twins are here in Ireland with us. But our eldest, Sam, decided to stay in England,' Kathleen explained. She passed the papers over to Dan to sign. 'I've been asking myself if we did the right thing. Sam was quite down when I spoke with him on the phone the other night.'

'Was he? You didn't tell me. What's wrong?' Dan asked sharply.

Kathleen swallowed.

'I'll tell you later, Dan,' she said quickly. She prickled with embarrassment under Liam's interested gaze. If only she'd found time earlier to speak to Dan about Sam.

Renewed tension fizzed in the air between them. They seemed to do nothing but snap at each other these days. All their plans of moving to Ireland, making a success of the hotel, and coming to terms with Dan's changed circumstances, seemed lost in the constant round of back-biting.

As if sensing the atmosphere, Liam changed the subject.

'And how are things going at the hotel?'

Dan frowned and Kathleen wished that Liam had picked a different subject.

'Well, it will take a while for us to find our feet, I expect,' she answered lamely, glancing sidelong at Dan.

'Yes. That's right,' he agreed tightly, rising awkwardly to his feet and bringing the meeting to a close.

'Thank you for your help, Liam. Now it's time we got back, I'm afraid. I have someone coming to see me this afternoon.'

Kathleen said her goodbyes, thankful to be leaving, and walked with Dan to the car, disturbed by the strain growing between them.

'I'm sorry, Dan,' she said when they were inside the vehicle.

'And when were you going to tell me, Kathleen?'

In the process of turning the ignition, Kathleen hesitated, surprised at the bitterness in Dan's voice.

'I . . . Dan, we've barely had a moment's peace to sit down and speak about anything. And, anyway, it's nothing desperate . . . it's just . . . '

'Just what?' Dan snapped.

'I don't know.' Kathleen heaved an exasperated sigh. She steered the car out of the school gates and headed for

154

home. 'Look, Dan, I spoke to him on the phone a few days ago. He sounded miserable and unhappy and I've been worried about him. I was going to talk to you about it, but I just haven't had the time.'

'I know things are hectic, Kathleen, but I would appreciate being included in what's happening to our children.'

'Oh, so now you're saying I'm excluding you!' Kathleen shook her head in frustration, lips tight shut. 'Well, now you know that Sam is having a bad time and maybe we shouldn't have left him on his own.'

Sighing, Dan rubbed his hand across his eyes. He was exhausted and wished the day was over.

'It's bound to take time to adjust, Kathleen. It was what he wanted.'

'So you don't care he's unhappy?' she accused him.

'Don't be ridiculous! Of course I care,' he snapped back, hurt. 'I'm just saying that Sam needs to be allowed to sort things out for himself. He'll ask if he needs us. We shouldn't go rushing in at the first sign of a problem.'

'If you weren't so wrapped up in the hotel all the time, perhaps we'd have more time to talk about things. A bit of communication goes a long way, you know.'

They drew to a halt in front of the faded facade of the hotel. Kathleen felt tears prick her eyes and, too late, wished she could call back her words.

'Well, thank you very much. If it's communication you want, then it's about time you realised that if we don't get to grips with our financial predicament, then we'll all be back in England with Sam. How's that for communication?'

Leaving her open-mouthed, Dan climbed painfully out of the car, slammed the door and limped across to the hotel.

Kathleen watched him go, wondering how long he had been keeping this from her. Would they ever regain the easy rapport they once shared?

A Prickly Character

'If you just wait a minute, I'll help you with that.'

'I don't need your help, thank you.' Hands on hips, Annie Webster flashed Stephen Fitzgerald an irritated glance. 'I'm quite capable of seeing to this myself. I do know what I'm doing.'

'Fine. Go right ahead.'

He lounged against the car and watched her, an amused smile playing on his lips. Annie turned on her heel and flounced down the bank towards the water's edge. The August sun beat down on her skin.

When Stephen had collected her from the airport, she had never imagined she would be stuck with him so much of the time. It wasn't as if she needed a babysitter, for goodness' sake. She was good at her job and she knew it. Granted, it had been helpful to have someone to show her the lie of the land, but now all she wanted was to be allowed to go about her work, without a chaperone — especially him.

But what was it about Stephen Fitzgerald that rubbed her up the wrong way? OK, so she hadn't been herself, she thought, since arriving in Ireland. The row she'd had with Neil, her boyfriend — ex-boyfriend, she reminded herself — had done nothing for her self-respect. And to come so soon before her departure from Canada — well, she seemed to have swapped one irritating, opinionated man for another!

Taking a deep breath, Annie paused for a moment to admire the scene around her. The rugged beauty and untamed wilderness of this place had gripped her from the first. Looking up at the hills, she saw clouds nestling at the jagged ridges, hiding them from full view. Soon these clouds would blot out the sun and bring a shower, at least.

'The weather changes so quickly, doesn't it?'

She hadn't noticed Stephen's approach.

His softly spoken question made her jump.

'Yes, it does,' she agreed, endeavouring to be civil.

'If you don't like the weather, wait a minute.'

Annie glanced at Stephen quizzically and he smiled.

'It's a local saying.'

Unexpectedly, Annie found herself smiling back.

'Right.'

She tried to concentrate on her work, sorting out her equipment, selecting bottles to collect the water samples she needed to test, all the while conscious of him, such a short distance away. She stole a quick look at him from beneath her lashes. He was handsome, sure enough, with his rakish dark hair, and impossibly blue eyes.

Frowning at the direction of her thoughts, she pulled herself up short and stepped forward towards the water. Stephen followed.

'At the risk of interfering,' he began.

She spun round to face him, catching the sparkle of amusement in his eyes.

'I . . . '

Before he could continue, Annie felt the ground slipping beneath her feet.

'Oooh!' she cried, the water bottles spilling from her hands as she reached out to steady herself.

As she balanced on the brink, fearful she was going to fall, Stephen reacted instinctively and reached for her, drawing her back from the crumbling edge of the bank. She cannoned into his arms and found herself tightly clasped against him. For a long moment they stood, horribly aware of the fascinating tingle of attraction rippling between them. Abruptly Annie pushed herself away from him, regaining control of the situation.

'Thank you,' she murmured awkwardly.

'No problem.'

Realising the powershift, Stephen held Annie's gaze until she looked away, uncomfortable at the longing she had found there.

Annie moved away and began to gather up her scattered bottles.

'Here, let me help you,' Stephen offered, taking some of the equipment from her. 'I was trying to tell you that the bank was safer farther along.'

'Thanks.' She bowed her head. Maybe he really had been trying to help after all.

Annie shoved her hair back from her face and let Stephen lead the way along the side of the lough to a place that gave much easier access to the cold, crystal water. She worked diligently, accepting Stephen's help to label and store the water samples. The silence between them was charged, but no longer hostile.

Annie was glad when they finished their work and headed back to the four-wheel-drive.

'Would you mind dropping me back at the hostel?' she asked once the samples were stored and she and Stephen were inside.

'Are you not coming for lunch?'

'Not today, I have some reports I need to finish up.' She excused herself with just a whisper of a lie. She needed some time alone to gather her head together. If she spent any longer in Stephen's company it would only add to her confusion.

★   ★   ★

Stephen was quiet on the drive back to the hostel, mulling over what had happened that morning. Annie had been so abrasive from the moment he had met her that he hadn't really looked at her as a woman before.

He allowed himself a quick glance at her stubborn profile and smiled. She was certainly a prickly character! But when she let go of her iron control she was revealed as a fascinating, fiery female. She intrigued him. Something had made her close in on herself. He had felt it when he had held her in his arms.

Pulling up outside the door to the hostel, the drizzle that had earlier threatened began to fall. Stephen waited as Annie gathered up her belongings.

'Would you mind taking the samples back to the centre for me?' she asked, minus her usual snippiness. 'I'll test them later this afternoon.'

'Sure.' He smiled.

For the second time that day Annie surprised him by smiling back.

'Thanks.'

'You're welcome.'

He met her gaze for several seconds, registering the uncertainty and unease which shadowed her eyes. He felt suddenly awkward and restarted the engine.

'See you later, then.'

Annie nodded, tiny beads of rain silvering her hair. She stepped back from the car and closed the door. Stephen watched as her trim figure ran towards the hostel.

He hadn't taken much interest in his social life since parting from Roisin at Easter. Something about Annie's mix of fire and ice was finding its way under his skin.

Swoon

'You're doing grand, Laura!' Fiona encouraged her friend as she settled her in the saddle, adjusted the stirrups and showed her how to hold the reins. 'How does it feel?'

'I'm not sure!'

Laura grinned down at Fiona's smiling face. It was the first time she had sat on a horse and it felt peculiar. As Fiona coaxed the placid brown mare forward, Laura clutched the front of Molly's saddle, frightened she would fall off.

'Just relax,' Fiona advised.

'You won't let go, will you?'

'Of course not! We'll just walk around for a while so you can get the feel of things.'

Scolding herself for being a wimp, Laura bit her tongue and tried to relax into the gentle rhythm of the horse's movement. Her fingers loosened their hold as she put her trust in Fiona.

She was glad she had come. It was the weekend before she and the twins would start their respective new schools for the first time. The thought scared her, especially after what had happened back in England. Laura was determined to put such worries from her mind — along with her concern about the strange atmosphere at home.

Over the last few days, her parents had been behaving very oddly and she wondered if they had had a row. There had certainly been some disagreement about Sam.

'Are you OK?'

Laura nodded as Fiona interrupted her reverie.

'This is great. I'm really enjoying it.'

'We'll soon have you riding as if you'd been born to it, just you wait and see!' Her friend laughed. 'It'll be grand to be able to go out hacking together. There are some gorgeous rides round here.'

By the time they arrived back in the stable-yard, Laura was sorry to have to dismount. She was sorrier still when she landed back on her feet and realised how wobbly and sore she felt.

'Crikey!' she yelped as Fiona led Molly into her stable and untacked her. 'I'm not sure I'll sit down again for a while!'

Fiona giggled.

'You'll toughen up soon, you'll see,' she promised, making sure Molly had fresh water and hay.

Laura moved forward to give Molly a pat. She loved the warm scent of horse, the silky coat soft under her fingers. If only she could have an animal of her own.

She'd been upset when her dad had explained it was too soon for her to have a puppy, and now all the litter had gone, except for Podge. He was gorgeous, shiny and black. But Fiona's family were keeping him.

Stifling her regret, she followed Fiona

outside, and watched as the other girl closed the door and tipped the lower kick-bolt shut with her foot.

'Come on, we'll go and see what Da's doing in the school. He said he'd be putting Declan and Paprika through their paces this morning.'

'OK.'

Happy just to be there, enjoying the sense of freedom and belonging, Laura walked along beside her friend to the outdoor school. As they approached, she could see a beautiful chestnut horse moving gracefully round the edge of the school at a controlled canter.

'He's beautiful,' she whispered to Fiona as they leaned against the rail.

'The horse or the rider?' Fiona grinned.

'I meant the horse!'

'Wait until you get a look at Declan then. He's seriously fit!'

Resting her head on her arms, Laura watched as horse and rider did a figure of eight through the arena, their pace slowing as they came to a halt beside

Jack Harrington. She couldn't hear what Fiona's dad said, but after a few moments, Declan urged the horse forward and lined up to take a couple of jumps in the centre of the school. They looked terribly big, Laura thought, her heart in her mouth, as the pair approached them, but they sailed over with inches to spare.

Eyes shining, she smiled at Fiona.

'That was great!'

'Da thinks they're going to do grand things together in a year or two. Paprika is fantastic. He's only five; still a baby. And Declan's just seventeen,' Fiona explained knowledgeably. 'Me da spotted Declan a couple of years ago. He comes from over near Dublin and his parents haven't much money, so Da offered to take him on when he left school.'

'Does he live with you then?'

'Not in the house. He's in the cottage with the yard manager and a couple of others.'

When the session came to an end,

Fiona took her arm and they walked back across the yard, standing aside as Paprika pranced past them, hooves clattering.

'I'll introduce you,' Fiona offered.

Laura stood at the stable door, watching while Declan untacked his horse, rubbed him down and made him comfortable. Still she hadn't had a good view of the young man Fiona was so enthusiastic about, for the peak of his riding helmet obscured his features.

'Hi, squirt,' he said when he turned and saw Fiona.

'Hi! Paprika's on fine form,' Fiona remarked.

'Aye, he's doing grand,' Declan agreed, his voice soft but husky. He took the saddle over his arm, the bridle in his hand and left the box, allowing Fiona to close the door for him.

'Thanks. And who's this?'

Laura held her breath as Declan turned to look at her, taking off his hat to release a shock of damp, dark hair.

Under the force of his gaze, she fought a sudden urge to step back, a flush warming her cheeks.

'This is Laura . . . I told you about her.'

Laura barely heard her friend's chatter as Fiona reminded Declan of the Jacksons' move to Ireland. She was conscious only of Declan's tall, lean frame as they walked together towards the tack-room, feeling him glance at her more than once from beneath luscious, dark eyelashes. He stowed the tack in place and turned to face her.

'I hope you'll be happy here.' He smiled.

'Thanks,' Laura murmured shyly. 'Everyone's been lovely.'

'Do you ride?'

'Fiona's trying to teach me. I had my first lesson today,' she explained, feeling ridiculously breathless.

Declan nodded and smiled again.

'Grand. Perhaps we can all go for a ride one day . . . when you've improved a bit.'

'I don't know,' Laura murmured, glancing at Fiona.

'We'll do that, Dec.' Her friend grinned. 'Laura's going to be a star. I know it!'

Laura swallowed as Declan's gaze lingered on hers, losing herself in the warmth of his coffee-brown eyes.

'I'll see you around,' he said, heading back across the stableyard.

'Isn't Declan just the business!' Fiona swooned and danced a twirl.

Her fervour made Laura laugh.

'He seemed nice.'

'Nice?' Fiona exclaimed, stopping to face Laura. 'He's drop dead gorgeous, Laura! Have you eyes in your head?'

As they went back to the house for some of their favourite coconut and lime ice-cream, Laura found her thoughts lingering on Declan. She'd never taken much interest in boys before, but something about him, about the way she had felt when he had looked at her, had released a thousand tiny butterflies inside her. It was a feeling she liked.

Kathleen hadn't enjoyed herself so much in ages. It was wonderful to hear the place filled with laughter. Most of all, it was great to see her family so relaxed and at ease. Her parents and Stephen were chatting happily with Teresa, Jack and Fiona. Only Sam was missing.

'That was grand, Kath.' Teresa grinned, helping carry the last of the things from the dining-room. 'You've inherited your ma's talent in the kitchen. That lamb was to die for! If yourself and Dan are going to treat your guests to food like that, you'll be doing a roaring trade!'

'Let's hope so.' Kathleen smiled, determined not to let worries about the hotel spoil this special Sunday. Tomorrow the children would start school and the official autumn season would begin. Her parents would be winding down and would spend less time helping out at the hotel. She and Dan would be left to their own devices.

As she carried a selection of sinful puddings through to the private dining-room, she was happy to find everyone laughing. She was just about to sit down and join them, when the bell rang at reception.

'Do you want me to go?' Dan asked, half rising from his chair.

Kathleen rested a hand on his shoulder and shook her head.

'I'll do it. You dish out.' She smiled.

Kathleen hurried to see who was there and was both surprised and delighted to find two couples from Switzerland looking to book in for a week. Dan would be pleased!

'We were not intending to stay,' one of the ladies explained, 'but the area is so beautiful that we changed our plans. Do you have room for us?'

'Yes, of course. I can offer you two double rooms with views of the hills.'

'That sounds marvellous,' the guests agreed.

Kathleen busied herself signing them

in then grabbed Stephen to assist with the luggage. Once she had seen them to their rooms, she hurried downstairs to ensure she had enough food out to cover the evening meals. That done, she went in search of her family.

Lunch over, her parents and Stephen had gone to sit outside with the twins. James was pleading with his grandpa to go fishing and Luke was talking excitedly about his next trip to the National Park with his uncle. Laura, Fiona and Teresa were walking round the garden, the puppy and his mother gambolling ahead of them towards the riverbank.

Filled with a sense of contentment and hope that things were about to improve, Kathleen smiled as she went back inside to find Dan.

A Dreadful Mistake

Voices from the dining-room attracted her attention and she walked down the carpeted corridor to the doorway. Dan and Jack, having apparently cleared the table and done the washing-up, were seated at the table over coffee. Kathleen hesitated, aware she was eavesdropping.

' . . . and the situation is more serious than I thought,' Dan was saying.

'I'm sure you can turn it around.' Jack tried to encourage him. 'Killarney has always been a magnet for tourists, and this place would be great again with some renovation.'

'Renovation isn't cheap, Jack.'

Jack frowned, taking a sip of his coffee.

'No, I know. But you get back what you put in. It worked for Teresa's family with the dairy.'

'I'm planning to set up a website, for online bookings. It would bring us into the twenty-first century. And at least it would be a start.'

'That's a great idea.'

'Let's hope so. But right now we need a miracle.'

'You've worked so hard, Dan, both of

you. And it's early days yet.'

Dan shook his head, running his fingers through his hair.

'But time and money are two things we haven't got. There's far more hard work and sacrifice ahead of us, Jack, if we're going to make a go of this, and the reality is that I'm in no physical shape to do it,' he continued, his words taking Kathleen completely by surprise.

'How do I tell Kathleen that I've let the family down? We've made a dreadful mistake coming here.'

6

A New Start

As the car drew up in front of the school, Laura felt positively ill with worry.

It was silly, she knew, but all those weeks ago, making plans to leave England, she hadn't considered the reality of attending school here. Now she had to make a new start in a class full of strangers — except for Fiona, of course. What if things turned out to be the same here?

Over the past few weeks she had enjoyed making friends with Fiona . . . and now Declan.

Her mother's voice cut in on her thoughts.

'Teresa and I had some smashing times here.' Kathleen gave her a reassuring hug. 'And you'll have Fiona to show you the ropes. I'm sure you'll love it.'

Laura felt raddled with doubt, but kept silent. And she had more than one anxiety to contend with. Yesterday, after lunch, her mum had gone all quiet and peculiar. Laura didn't like it when things she didn't understand went on at home.

'Come on, pet, off you go.' Kathleen's tone was edged with impatience, and it brooked no argument. Reluctantly, Laura reached for her bag. 'Have a good day, now.'

'Bye,' Laura muttered ungraciously, slipping out of the car.

As her mother drove away, she looked up dismally at the building. She didn't want to go inside. Tears stung her eyes.

She debated what to do, watching nervously as cars came and went and girls of varying ages spilled out and headed into school, chatting and laughing as they caught up on the gossip. Suddenly, she heard Fiona's voice.

'Laura! You're here! It's awful on the first day, isn't it?'

Laura nodded, worried she would embarrass herself by crying.

'Sure, it really is OK here, honest!' Fiona grinned, linking her arm through Laura's.

'Let's away in. We've to see Sister Phil before assembly.'

Laura tried to control her nausea as she walked with Fiona down the citrus-scented corridors. She had found the headmistress intimidating when she had met her with Kathleen to look round the school. But this morning, entering Sister Philomena's inner sanctum, the tall, graceful nun, wisps of grey hair escaping from beneath her wimple, rose from behind her desk with a warm and welcoming smile.

'Laura!' Her dark eyes twinkled merrily. 'It's good to see you again.'

'Thank you, Sister,' Laura said hoarsely.

'Sit down, the pair of you.' The head gestured, with a little nod, to two chairs in front of her desk.

'Whatever will become of me, having you two girls together here? I suppose you've heard all about your mothers' escapades when they were your age?'

Responding to the headmistress's warmth, Laura smiled and shook her head. Beside her, Fiona grinned.

'What a terrible pair! Kathleen Fitzgerald and Teresa O'Connor. Is it any surprise my hair turned white?' Sister Phil lamented, making the girls giggle. 'And now I have their daughters in my school!'

'We'll be models of propriety, Sister,' Fiona insisted, straight-faced.

Sister Phil grinned, revealing a gap in her upper teeth.

'Do I look like I came down with the last shower, young lady? Still, it's to be hoped that Laura here may be a good influence on you!'

Laura glanced at Fiona, caught the mischievous girl's wink, and stifled another giggle.

'Now, Laura,' the headmistress continued soberly. 'I know it will be strange adjusting to a different school — not to mention a new educational system

— but I feel you will do well here. At least, at your age, you'll be spared learning Gaelic, unlike your younger brothers! It wasn't one of your mother's favourite subjects, if I remember rightly. Now, is there anything you want to ask me?'

Laura bit her lip.

'I don't think so, Sister.'

'I know what happened before, Laura, and I can promise you there will be none of that sort of thing in my school.' She smiled kindly at Laura, resting a comforting hand on her arm. 'We're just one big family here. Everyone is expected to work hard, but all are treated with respect. I know Fiona will look after you. And if you have any worries whatsoever, my door is always open. Understood?'

'Yes, Sister. Thank you,' Laura added shyly.

'Good. Off you go then, both of you. And no running in the corridors!'

Fiona led Laura briskly from the office.

'She's not a bad old stick, is she?'

'Fiona!'

'Well, it's true! She can be as tough as old boots, but she has a heart of gold, has Sister Phil.'

The noise of girlish voices grew louder as they approached the hall, increasing in volume as Fiona pushed open the doors. Self-consciousness suddenly gripped Laura as she followed Fiona to a row of chairs that held the other members of their class.

'This is Laura.' Fiona introduced her to her classmates amidst a babble of chatter.

By the time the teachers, led by Sister Philomena, arrived on the small stage at one end of the hall and silence descended, Laura's nerves had begun to abate. Maybe this really would be a whole new start.

Time Off

'Brian, do you have a moment?' Sam asked, hesitating at the door of his boss's office. 'Could I have a word?'

'Of course, come in.' The older man smiled.

Sam closed the door and walked towards the cluttered desk, wondering how Brian ever found anything he needed in all the mess. He waited patiently as his employer finished filling in the details on an MOT test certificate and embossed the paper with the official garage stamp.

'What can I do for you?'

'I know I've only been working full-time for three months, but I was wondering if it would be OK for me to have a few days off,' Sam explained, surprised at how nervous he was.

Brian raised one bushy, salt and pepper eyebrow as he sat forward and searched in the rubble for his diary.

'When did you have in mind?' he asked, frowning.

'Maybe next week?'

'I don't know . . . ' The ringing of the telephone interrupted his reply and Brian gestured to a nearby chair. 'Take

a seat, Sam. I must answer this
— Avril's at the bank.'

'I Miss My Family'

Hiding his frustration, Sam did as he
was told. He closed his eyes briefly, and
realised how desperately he wanted
Brian to say yes. He didn't feel any
better about things since his phone
conversation with his mum, and he'd
had another disappointing weekend
with Nicola.

Was it unfair of him, he asked
himself, to want to spend time with
her? True, she had two years of A-levels
ahead, and he knew how important it
was for her to be successful in obtaining
the grades she needed for vet school,
but surely they could still have some
fun?

Sam bit his lip. They had rowed when
she had cancelled yet another date.
Aside from his problems with Nicola,
he felt generally dissatisfied.

The friends he had been close to all his young life were either staying on at school, had gone away to college, or were just lazing around. He was the only one working, and he often felt that in three short months a chasm had appeared between him and his peers. They seemed so young and immature. At least he had his football, now the cricket season was over.

'Sorry about that,' Brian apologised, replacing the receiver. 'Now, about that time off.'

Sam looked across at him, hope in his eyes.

'Is it OK for me to go?'

'Go where?'

'I mean, to have the days off?' Sam said.

Steepling his fingers under his chin, Brian regarded him curiously.

'Are you having problems, Sam? Is there anything I can help you with?'

'No,' Sam said bravely. 'I'm OK.'

'You do know you can come to me, or Avril, if you need anything?'

'Yeah, sure.'

Brian watched as the young man's gaze slid away, teeth nibbling anxiously at his lip. Something wasn't right, that was for sure, and he'd promised Sam's parents he would take care of him.

'It's not easy, is it, living on your own for the first time?' he asked, looking back at the diary in front of him and wondering if they could cope without the boy for a few days.

Sam shrugged.

'I suppose not,' he murmured, raising his uneasy gaze to find Brian watching him.

'You've been doing a good job, Sam. I know it's frustrating for you, wanting to get on and do more on the racing side. But, first off, we have to get you your provisional and, anyway, the season's almost over. We'll be doing some testing over the winter and I was thinking we could start you off on that.'

Sam nodded and tried to muster the kind of enthusiasm such an offer would have roused in him just a few weeks ago.

'That would be good, thanks.'

'You're seventeen at the end of the month, aren't you?'

'Yes. I have everything filled in for my provisional licence — and the theory test.'

Brian looked at him speculatively.

'And what about day release at college?'

'That's on a Tuesday,' Sam pointed out, having been prepared for this argument. 'I was hoping to go off on the Tuesday night or Wednesday morning.'

'And this time off is important to you?' Brian probed, troubled by how miserable the boy seemed.

Sam nodded, his tone and expression adamant.

'It is.'

'So, if I say yes, what is it you have in mind to do? You know we're short-staffed at the moment. Are you off for a cheap break in sunnier climes with that girl of yours?'

'Chance would be a fine thing.' Sam

tried to joke in response to the teasing and a silence stretched between them. Feeling suddenly like a little boy again, instead of the man he thought he was, Sam swallowed down a sudden rush of emotion.

'I miss my family,' he admitted unsteadily. 'I need to see them . . . I need to talk to my dad.'

Grand

'How did it go?' Dan asked his children, when they arrived home from their first day in their new schools.

'I had a grand time.' Luke grinned, still looking smart and neat in his new uniform. 'We all had to write about what we'd done over the summer and then stand up in front of the class and read out our essays. I wrote about being in the National Park with Uncle Stephen,' he chattered on excitedly. 'Miss Lacey said my work was excellent.'

'That's great, Luke.' His father laughed, ruffling his hair.

James looked on with a scowl. Typical Luke! He was glad he hadn't had to stand up in front of the whole class. Everything always came so easily to Luke. It just wasn't fair.

He remembered what Gramps had told him on one of their fishing trips.

'You and Luke are just good at different things.'

Compared to Luke, he never felt good enough. But today hadn't been so bad.

'How was your day, James?' his mother asked, smiling at him as she put some glasses of milk and a plate of biscuits on the kitchen table.

James helped himself to a cookie.

'I had a grand time, too. Mr Flanagan isn't a bit like a headteacher. And my form master, Mr Murphy, is really cool,' he told them.

'What did you do then?' Luke asked, surprised. What had been going on at this new school to make his twin so keen all of a sudden?

James stuffed another chocolate biscuit in his mouth and grinned.

'We did the usual boring stuff like maths, English and history, but in the afternoon, we played football. My side won and I scored a goal! Then we did woodwork.

'It was great, Dad. I love it. I'm learning to make things like you do.'

Delighted that the boy had taken so readily to his new environment, Dan gave James a big hug, ignoring the twinge of pain in his back.

'I'm really proud of you . . . both of you,' he said, drawing Luke into his embrace as well.

'Away up and get changed now,' Kathleen reminded her boys.

Smiling as the twins clattered noisily up the back stairs, talking all the while, she turned to Laura.

'What about you, pet?' she asked as she began to make preparations for the evening meal.

'It wasn't as bad as I expected,' Laura

admitted. She moved to her father's side and hugged him, earning an encouraging squeeze in return. 'Sister Phil was kind and the girls in class were nice. The lessons were good, too, and I wasn't as out of touch with the work as I thought I might be.'

Dan was relieved this awkward first day was over for his sensitive daughter. He caught Kathleen's gaze, his own emotions mirrored in her eyes.

'You've done really well, Laura,' he praised her. 'I know how hard today was for you.'

Laura beamed at him.

'Thanks, Dad.' She skipped off to change, promising to come back down and lay the tables for dinner.

'Can I do anything to help you in here?' Dan asked, rising stiffly to his feet.

'No, I'm fine.' Turning her head to look at him, Kathleen smiled tentatively. 'Thanks, though.'

Dan smiled back, hoping the distance between them was slowly beginning to close again.

'OK. I'll be in the office if you need me.'

Kathleen watched him go. She wondered if she should tell him she had overheard his admission the day before. She knew she had been a bit off with him after catching him confiding in Jack, and she knew he sensed the change in her. Hadn't he told her often enough that things were worse than she thought? The trouble was that the realisation had only sunk in when she had heard the utter despair in his voice.

She couldn't let him fail. After all, it wasn't only Dan's fault, and it wasn't just his dream, either. Today had been a new start for Laura and the boys — they couldn't take that away from them. Somehow, she and Dan had to find a way to make this work.

Drenched

'Stephen! Stop the car!' Jamming on the brakes, Stephen brought the car to a halt at the side of the road.

'What's the matter? What's happened?' he demanded, a cold sweat beading his brow.

'I thought so!' His mother, sitting in the passenger seat, peered through the steamy side window, out at the rainswept pavement. Satisfied, she nudged her son in the ribs.

'Get out and help her.'

'What are you talking about?' he complained.

'Your girl — Annie, isn't it? She's getting a drenching,' Mary told her son.

Cursing under his breath, Stephen stepped out into the rain and rounded the car. Sure enough, Annie was walking along the pavement, huddled into her jacket. Only she wasn't his girl! How on earth had his mother spotted her in this weather?

'Hop in,' he called as Annie drew level. He opened the door and shoved his mother's shopping across the back seat.

Annie hesitated, clearly uncertain.

With the rain running down his neck, Stephen shifted impatiently.

'Come on,' he said sharply. 'I'm drowning here!'

He didn't catch what Annie muttered, which was probably just as well. He hurried back round the car and got behind the steering-wheel, snapped on his seatbelt, feeling the rain seep through his clothes, and drove on in silence, allowing his mother to carry on the conversation.

'I couldn't let you walk all that way in this weather,' Mary explained, swivelling in her seat to smile at the girl in the back. 'As soon as I spotted you, I told Stephen to stop!'

'Thank you.'

Annie had to admit she was grateful to be out of that sudden downpour, even if her rescuer was the last person she would have chosen.

'You don't mind if Stephen drops me off first, do you? Only I really have to get this frozen stuff put away.'

'Of course not,' Annie agreed politely,

minding very much.

Glancing up, she met Stephen's gaze in the rearview mirror and saw that for once they were in full agreement. She couldn't help but smile inwardly, realising that he was as put out as she was.

'She Likes To Meddle'

By the time they were driving up the hill and along Aghadoe Heights towards the Fitzgeralds' new bungalow, the wind had blown away the sudden shower and a shaft of sunlight was streaming through the clouds. It lit the ridge of MacGuillycuddy's Reeks and danced on the waters of the lough.

'It's a beautiful spot you have up here, Mrs Fitzgerald,' Annie complimented Mary, helping to hand the supermarket carrier-bags out of the back of the car.

'Grand, isn't it?' The older woman beamed. 'Come on, now. You must come away in and have a look, now you're here. I'll put the kettle on. We can have a cup of tea and you can dry out while I wait for Kevin to come back from fishing.'

It was an hour before they could escape, and Stephen wasn't sure whether to be annoyed or amazed. In the short time they had been sitting round the table, watching dusk fall over the view outside, his mother had discovered more about Annie Webster than he had learned since her arrival in Ireland.

'I'm sorry about Ma,' he apologised when they were back in the car and heading to town. 'She likes to meddle.'

'I thought she was charming.' Annie smiled. She had felt so at home in the Fitzgeralds' house that she really hadn't minded Mary's probing at all.

'She gave you a bit of a grilling. She should have been a detective!'

'I'm sure she means well.'

Stephen kept his feelings to himself on that one.

'I'd be interested to hear about your studies in Canada some time,' he said, throwing her a quick glance.

'Such as?' Annie was glad the shadows masked her expression.

'I've always been interested in Killarney Provincial Park, but I've never had the opportunity to visit. I read some articles in a magazine about pollution from the smelter, and how it was affecting the water and aquatic life.'

Surprised at his awareness, Annie nodded.

'Yes, that's right, and it's part of my research. There have been a lot of problems with the superstack at Sudbury, which is the largest town in that area of Ontario.

'The emissions of copper, nickel and sulphur dioxide from the smelter spread out over the district, including the Whitefish Lake Indian Reserve and the Killarney Provincial Park, almost sixty kilometres away. The water quality is improving but it's taken a lot of hard work, and there are still numerous environmental problems.'

Stephen's interest grew and he was caught by the way Annie's reserve disappeared as she talked with enthusiasm about her work and her home environment. As he drew up in front of the hostel, he switched off the engine and turned in his seat to face her.

'Perhaps you'd care to come out for a drink one night?' he ventured cautiously. 'I am serious about wanting to learn more about your research — and about the similarities between our two parks.'

'I'd like that,' she agreed. She surprised herself by throwing caution to the wind and accepting his invitation. 'Thank you.'

'Great! Perhaps next weekend?'

'OK.'

In the early evening darkness Stephen met her gaze, his blue eyes studying her intently. She felt a flickering in her stomach that brought alarm and excitement in equal measure.

'Thanks for the lift,' she murmured,

fumbling for the door catch.

'No problem. I'm sorry it was a roundabout one.'

Annie returned his infectious smile.

'At least it was dry . . . And I had a nice cup of tea!' She laughed, opening the door and slipping out.

'See you, Annie.'

'See you,' Annie replied.

She felt strangely lighthearted as she walked smartly towards the hostel.

Hope

The weekend was a hectic one. Kathleen was grateful that the children were occupied elsewhere, allowing her to organise the staff and chores and plan the meals, while Dan dealt with guests, bills and other problems.

Laura and the twins had completed their first week at their respective new schools with as much enthusiasm as they had shown on their first day, and Kathleen was inordinately relieved. It could have been an entirely different story.

Now James was spending the morning with his grandparents before going on to a school friend's party that afternoon. Luke had joined a music group at his school and Stephen had promised to pick him up at lunch-time and take him to the park. As for Laura, she had dashed off as soon as breakfast was over to spend the day with Fiona at the riding stables.

Kathleen smiled as she worked alongside Josie in the kitchen. At least one aspect of life here was on an even keel.

Back in the office, Dan finished sorting out the bills for the guests who would leave that morning, before turning his attention to the post. The usual invoices continued to pile up with frightening regularity. At least they had had a fresh influx of guests that morning: an unexpected booking from a family visiting from America, a couple of cyclists looking for a weekend break and an elderly couple from Scotland who wanted a nostalgic holiday in the town where they had spent their honeymoon, forty-five years previously.

Dan filed the invoices ready for attention and opened the rest of the post. There were a few other enquiries and requests for brochures. If only, he thought, he could find time to finish the website. The increased publicity would surely bring in more bookings. He had to keep up the momentum if the business was to succeed.

The last envelope he came to looked official. His heart sank when he opened it and found it was from the bank. But as he read, a sensation of hope grew inside him and the sinking feeling lifted.

'Kath?' he called, rising stiffly to his feet and heading to the kitchen. 'Kathleen!'

'What's wrong?' Kathleen asked, meeting him in the reception area.

'I'm not sure,' he said, leaning heavily on the counter. 'Look. Read this.'

He showed her the letter, scanning her face as she read. Finally, she looked up at him, hope in her eyes.

'Do you think it's good news?' she asked in disbelief.

'Your guess is as good as mine. But it's interesting that she wants to meet us. If what it says is true,' he continued, trying not to get too carried away, 'and if the old business manager, who turned us down, has retired, then there's certainly no harm in meeting this new woman. If we play our cards right we could get just the loan we need to carry out the essential renovations.'

'Oh, Dan!'

'Let's hope we can convince this Ms O'Rourke when she comes to see us next week,' he finished, unable to hide his relief.

Rounding the desk gingerly, he took Kathleen in his arms, hopeful that at last they could turn things around. He pulled back to meet her gaze and was heartened by a new brightness in her eyes.

'I know things haven't been easy, but we won't give up, Kath. I promise.'

The telephone interrupted their intimacy.

'Good morning, Waterside Hotel,' Dan said, answering. He caught Kathleen's hand to prevent her departure when he realised who was on the other end of the line.

'Hi, Dad.'

'Sam! It's great to hear your voice, son. How are things?'

'Not too bad.'

Dan detected the uncertainty Sam tried to mask.

'Are you all OK?'

'We're fine.' Dan shared a smile with his wife. 'Your mum's just here. Do you want to talk to her?'

'In a minute. Listen, Dad, I have a few days off next week. Would it be OK if I came over?'

'That would be fantastic, Sam! We'd love to see you. Do you need me to send you some money?'

'It's all sorted.' Sam laughed. 'I checked the cheap airlines on the internet and I've booked a flight from

203

Stansted to Kerry — it's easier than Cork or Shannon. Can someone pick me up on Wednesday?'

'Just try and stop us! Give me the details and then I'll hand you over to your mother, before she explodes.'

Feeling lighter than he had in a long time, Dan looked forward to enjoying the weekend.

It had been frantic, Kathleen allowed as Sunday afternoon arrived. Every expected guest had turned up, and there had even been a couple of last-minute bookings, one sent down from the National Park thanks to Stephen, and one an enquiry through the tourist office in town.

She and Josie had had a hectic time in the kitchen catering for them all; they'd had to order an extra delivery from Teresa at the dairy. Despite the time of year, her special ice-creams were still popular, especially with five of the six Americans. The final member of their party, a vegan, ate no meat, fish or dairy products.

The wet autumn day had confined many visitors to the hotel. Several of the Americans still appeared to be suffering from jet lag. Kathleen felt desperately sad for them, the nature of their trip being the funeral of an elderly relative, which they were due to attend in a couple of days' time.

'We had such a happy new baby party for my niece back home in New York just days ago,' the mother, Nancy Dooley, had explained after breakfast that morning. 'And here we are now marking the passing of my husband's grandmother.'

Kathleen felt a welling of sympathy for the family.

'It's very sad. I'm so sorry.'

'It's the cycle of life,' the other woman responded philosophically.

Kathleen glanced up from preparing vegetables as Dan came into the kitchen. Seeing the worry on his face, she set down the knife.

'Is something wrong?'

'I hope not.' A frown creased his

forehead. 'It's the Dooleys.'

'What about them?'

'Several of them are complaining of stomach cramps and sickness. It seems to have come on quite quickly. I said I'd ask you to pop up and talk with Mrs Dooley before I called the doctor.'

Anxiety gripped her as she stared at Dan.

'It's not that serious, surely?'

'They're saying it's something they ate here, Kath,' Dan said sternly, his concern evident. 'The only one who's feeling fine is the girl, Manda. She said she's the only one who hasn't eaten any of the dairy food or meat.'

'It can't be,' Kath whispered.

'Well, we have to do something. Will you go up and have a word first?'

'Yes, of course.' She pressed her hands to her cheeks, hoping against hope it would turn out not to be serious. 'I'll go now.'

'And I'd better look out the doctor's phone number,' Dan announced grimly.

A Distressing Situation

Two hours later, the situation seemed to be snowballing out of control.

'It's possible at least one of them will have to be admitted to hospital, I'm afraid,' the doctor announced, updating Kathleen and Dan in the office. 'I'm sorry, but it shows all the signs of food poisoning, and I am going to have to report it to the environmental health people.'

'We understand,' Kathleen murmured, an unbearable knot of anxiety tightening inside her.

Pale and distressed, Dan rose to see the man out.

'Thank you for coming, Doctor.'

'That's OK, Mr Jackson. I'll call back a bit later to see how things are. Try not to worry now.'

Easier said than done, Dan thought to himself as he limped back into the office. He halted in the doorway. Kathleen sat with her head in her hands. She looked up at him, tears blurring her eyes.

Just when things had started to look up for them, the rug had been pulled from under their feet. And it could mean the end of all they had been working towards . . .

7

Under Threat

By Monday morning, officialdom had swung into action. Kathleen felt over-whelmed by the whole proceedings; concerned both for the guests who were ill, and the disastrous implications for the hotel's future.

Mrs Dooley had been taken to hospital, but the other members of the family remained in their rooms, cared for by Kathleen and Manda Dooley. It seemed that Manda, who was a vegan, had not eaten whatever had brought on the painful cramps and illness in the rest of her family. The district nurses were making regular visits, and keeping Dr Moran informed.

'We must keep up the fluids,' the doctor had firmly asserted on his first visit. 'Hopefully we'll have some news on the samples I've taken before too long, but it might be a few days before they're back from the lab. The Environment Health Officer and the Area Medical Officer will be in touch.'

The efficient but frightening-sounding Outbreak Control Team had descended upon them later that morning, and were in the throes of inspecting the kitchen and taking specimens for testing.

Kathleen hoped with all her heart the tests would be clear. The last thing they needed was an outbreak and the ensuing implications. So far, no other guests had fallen ill, and neither the staff nor her own family had been affected. But one worrying aspect was the way Teresa's dairy had been dragged into the investigation as a suspect source. Now Teresa had arrived to confront Kathleen.

'So you think I've been supplying you with contaminated food?'

Teresa had been understandably alarmed when an Environmental Health Officer and clinical microbiologist had arrived at the dairy early that morning. She stood defiantly, arms crossed, as she glared at Kathleen.

'Of course we don't suspect you.' Kathleen tried to reassure her friend, but tiredness and anxiety brought an uncharacteristic snap to her voice. 'It isn't much fun for us, either, Teresa. You can see for yourself what's going on. We have no idea what has caused this illness. It's out of our hands. Doctor Moran had no option but to report the problem. And we have been obliged to give details of all our suppliers to the authorities. I'm sure it's only precautionary.'

'And that makes it all right?'

'No. Of course it's not all right,' Kathleen protested. She was so annoyed with Teresa's selfish attitude that she couldn't help the irritation which laced her voice. 'These people are just doing their jobs, Teresa. I'm sure everything will be fine in a day or two.'

'So much for friendship!'

Kathleen blanched as Teresa turned

on her heel and flounced out of the back door.

Shaking her head, Kathleen returned to the storeroom, where a harassed Josie and a pale-faced Dan were answering the EHO's questions.

'And no-one else has shown any signs of illness?' the man asked again. He took copious notes, everything about him pristine.

'No-one,' Dan confirmed.

The man nodded thoughtfully.

'I'd be grateful if you could contact any guests who have been here in the last week and ask them to report any signs of sickness to you.'

'All right,' Dan agreed, his expression grim. 'I'll get started on that right away. Can I ask what happens now, though? What about the other guests we have, and those booked in during the next few days? And what about any publicity? Word of this would be very bad for our business — and for our suppliers, too.'

'I understand, Mr Jackson. I can

assure you we certainly won't be alerting the media, not at this stage, anyway. As for the immediate future, the initial inspection of the premises has been completed and we are satisfied so far with the standards here.

'I don't believe the premises present a grave danger to public health so we won't be shutting you down. You can carry on with your current bookings, but I will need to monitor your operations and talk to the rest of the staff, guests and family.

'We'll also have to await the results of tests to isolate the bacteria causing the illness, and that could take a few days.'

It all sounded horrendous, Kathleen thought as Dan left the kitchen to contact recent guests, though the EHO seemed satisfied with their storage procedures and general hygiene and preparation standards. Kathleen, eager to help in any way she could, was still smarting over Teresa's reaction to the crisis.

'I've taken samples of the leftover food from yesterday's meal and I have a list of what the poorly guests remember eating,' the EHO explained. 'Can you tell me what your own family and any of the staff had to eat, please?'

Kathleen went through the details with him, pressing her fingers to her forehead where a tension headache was gathering.

'The only staff are Josie, Maeve and Bridget. But Maeve and Bridget don't have any rôle in the handling and preparation of food, and they finished at lunchtime yesterday, so they would only have had their coffee break. And you've already spoken to Josie.'

'I know all this is very distressing for you and your husband, Mrs Jackson, but we need to be thorough in our investigations.'

'Yes, we understand that.'

'Please be extra vigilant. If you have any problems or suspicions, please get in touch with me straightaway. I'll be back, of course, and will let you have the results of the tests just as soon as they are available.'

'Thank you.'

As the team of officials left, Kathleen returned to the kitchen and filled herself a glass of water, taking a couple of paracetamol from the medicine kit in the cupboard. She sat at the table and swallowed the tablets.

Could this nightmare get any worse?

Changes

'How long will you be gone?'

'Only a few days,' Sam replied, surprised and secretly pleased that Nicola seemed disconcerted by his forthcoming trip. He continued packing his few things into the bag lying open on the bed. 'I'll be back on Sunday or Monday.'

'It's a bit sudden, isn't it?' Nicola complained.

'I want to see my family, that's all. The opportunity came up for a few days off.'

Nicola sat down on the edge of the bed and flicked some loose strands of glossy dark hair back over her shoulder.

'Are you missing them more than you thought?'

'Maybe.' Sam sighed, not wishing to reveal the true extent of his emotions. 'It's been a while since they moved and I'd just like to see them, especially my dad.'

He glanced up at Nicola and saw the pout on her face. Perhaps it was a good thing for him to do something unexpected now and again, he mused as he zipped the bag closed. After all, he seemed to have done all the running in the past few weeks. She had cancelled several dates because something more important had come up.

'There. I'm all ready.' He smiled. 'I've an early start in the morning, so shall we go out and have something to eat?'

'OK.'

It pleased Sam that Nicola seemed to make more of an effort that evening. He realised it was the first time they had spent alone together in ages. But the feeling of a shift in their relationship remained. As he walked her home, she linked her arm with his, pressing close to him. The lights were on in the front room of her house, signifying the presence of her parents, so they halted outside.

'You will be coming back, won't you?' she asked softly.

'Of course I will.'

'I know things haven't been great lately, Sam, but I'll miss you.'

Smiling, Sam cupped her face in his hands and kissed her.

'I'll see you in a few days.'

As the plane came in to land at County Kerry, Sam still felt half asleep. He wasn't good at early starts and had needed to set off at an obscene hour to make the journey to Stansted for his flight. But now he was here, excitement bubbled within him at the prospect of seeing his family again.

The formalities complete, he hoisted his bag over his shoulder and followed the trickle of passengers towards the meeting point. He scanned the faces impatiently in the Arrivals area, searching for his mother or father. He was sure one of them would come to meet him and he couldn't wait to see them. When he finally spotted the grinning faces of his grandparents, however, he experienced a rush of disappointment.

'You look grand!' Mary exclaimed, hugging him. 'How was your flight?'

'Fine.' Sam smiled and kissed her. His grandad slapped him heartily between the shoulder blades.

'Hi, Gramps.'

'Good to see you, Sam.'

'Your mum and dad send their love, pet,' his gran explained as they walked towards the exit. 'They had planned to come and collect you themselves, but there's been a bit of bother at the hotel.'

Sam frowned.

'What's happened?'

'A few guests were taken ill on Sunday night. The environmental health people have been in and things are a bit hectic,' Kevin said, helping stow the bag in the boot of the car. 'I'm sure it will blow over in a few days, but it's obviously a worrying time for them.'

'Why didn't they say?'

As his grandfather started the engine and steered the car towards the Killarney road, his grandmother adjusted her seatbelt and turned to smile at him.

'They didn't want to worry you. Sure, we've all been so excited at the thought of seeing you.'

Sitting back, Sam watched the passing scenery, reflecting on his plans for his visit. He was worried, naturally, for his parents and what this latest setback would mean for their business. But he was also frustrated. He had been so looking forward to this break, and desperate to discuss things with his dad. Now it looked as if his parents would be preoccupied.

Attraction

Stephen walked off the hill after a long but satisfying day. Behind him, the peaks of MacGillicuddy's Reeks were hidden by low cloud. The sunshine which had highlighted the orangey-red bracken was giving way to that gun metal grey which experience told him would bring rain.

Rain made him think of Annie and the thawing of the chill between them a few days ago, when his ma had made him stop to give the young woman a lift. He hadn't seen much of her since.

His own work had taken him up on the hills, where he most enjoyed being, while Annie had busied herself with her project round the lakes, either alone or with help from one of the other rangers. Try as he might to deny it, Stephen missed her fiery company.

Crossing over Brickeen, he walked through the woods, where red squirrels scampered, gathering stores for the long winter ahead. The leaves of the trees were beginning to turn with the changing season. He strode on towards Muckross. As he was passing the hostel, he saw Annie sitting on a bench by the lake, her head tilted as she listened to the eerie noises echoing off the hills. Adjusting his rucksack, he changed direction and walked towards her.

'It's an amazing sound, isn't it?'

Annie jumped when she heard his voice, spinning round to face him, watching as he closed the last of the distance between them. A spark of awareness tingled through her; part of her wanted to keep him at a distance, but another part could not deny her attraction to him.

'Yes,' she agreed.

'It stirs me every year,' Stephen admitted, sitting beside her and listening to the red deer stags whose distant bellows proclaimed the annual rut was underway.

'Did you know the Killarney herd are the only wild native red deer left in Ireland?'

Annie's steely-grey eyes sparked with interest.

'No, I didn't realise that. You have Sika deer in the park, too, though.'

'We do, but they're an exotic

introduction and can cause problems with overgrazing, not to mention diluting the genetic purity of the red deer.'

'And the Sika are the ones who have been keeping me awake at night?'

Stephen laughed.

'Probably! The Sika rut tends to start a week or two before the reds, and their high-pitched wails can be pretty spooky!'

'I noticed!' She swept some wisps of her streaky blonde fringe away from her eyes. 'I met your mother in town yesterday. She told me about the problems at the hotel. Is there any news?'

'I spoke with my sister, Kathleen, last night and the good thing is that no-one else has fallen ill. They're waiting for lab results just now. It's been a grim time right enough,' he finished, shaking his head.

'I'm sure it will all be sorted out soon.'

He smiled again, grateful for her reassurance.

'All being well.'

They sat in companionable silence for a few moments, enjoying the stillness and the wildlife around them.

'I'd best be on my way. I'm due in at the education centre before I finish up,' he said. Rising to his feet, he hitched his rucksack back in place then hesitated.

'Listen, I meant what I said the other day about that drink and learning more about your work and home turf.'

'OK.' Annie glanced up at him, her smile nervous. 'This weekend?'

He looked away across the water as the dusk began to close in, unable to meet her gaze.

'How about I pick you up here at the hostel — seven-thirty on Saturday night?'

'Sure. That'll be fine.'

The arrangement made, Stephen hiked on round the sweeping horseshoe curve of Castlelough Bay and back towards town, wondering if he was all kinds of fool.

* * *

'Are you OK walking down here?'

Dan smiled at his eldest son, relishing his company, if only for a short while.

'It's good for me to get some gentle exercise each day.'

'How are you really, Dad?'

'I'm OK.'

Sam gave a disbelieving sigh and sat down on a bench that afforded a stunning view of the hills basking in the autumn sunshine.

'Dad, I'm not stupid. I can see things are difficult with the hotel. But you look so tired and worried — and you seem in as much pain now as you were before you left England. I thought the point of this venture was to improve your health, not destroy it?'

'It was . . . is. It just takes time, and the initial start-up has been more fraught than we anticipated.' Dan paused, watching his son, a slow smile spreading across his face

'What?' Sam asked, puzzled at the

look in his father's eyes.

'You've grown up so much these last months. Your mum and I are proud of you, you know.'

'Dad!' He shot his father a sidelong glance, as he felt the blush creeping up his cheeks.

Dan smiled again, patting his son fondly on the back.

'It's true. I'm sure things haven't been easy for you, either, but I admire you for sticking at it. We certainly wouldn't have been having this kind of talk a little while ago, would we?'

'No. I guess not.' Sam looked down at the ground, scuffing the toe of one battered trainer in the loose dirt that edged the path. 'The thing is though, Dad, I'm not sure I really know what I do want any more.'

'Do you want to talk about it?'

Sam looked openly at his father.

'I think so. It was why I wanted to come — to talk. But I didn't know then that you were under so much pressure. I don't want to add to it, Dad.'

'You won't be.' Dan smiled. 'Don't be daft, lad. You know I'm always here for you.'

'I know,' Sam mumbled, gazing out towards the hills.

'So, is it work, or Nicola — or something else?' Dan could sense his son's reserve and did his best to encourage Sam to relax and confide in him.

Sam drew in a lungful of clear mountain air.

'A bit of everything, really. I was so sure I could make a go of things, convinced I was doing the right thing staying in England. I know it sounds silly, but I didn't expect to miss you all so much.'

'Aaah! The arrogance of youth!' Dan declared. 'I remember it well.'

Seeing his dad's grin, Sam chuckled quietly.

'Yeah, maybe. But maybe I'm just plain dumb.' He ran his hands over his face, rubbing the tension from his eyelids.

'You were never dumb, Sam. So, tell me what's been happening.'

'It's just been harder living on my own in that flat than I thought it would be. Brian and Avril have been great and they seem pleased enough with my work at the garage, but . . . ' Sam began to open up about the job, and how he wasn't enjoying it as much as he had thought.

'It was fun working there in the holidays and at weekends, but day in, day out it's boring. It doesn't help that I don't have my licence, but even when I do it will be a long time before I can expect to do anything on the racing side. I don't even know if I fancy that any more. But . . . '

Dan waited, reflecting on what Sam had said, while his son sought the right words.

'But?' he prompted after a few seconds.

'I don't know. It's just not how I thought it would be. I know I'm not academic. I thought being a mechanic would suit me. But even though it's not been long, I'm just not so sure now.

'I'll tell you what is surprising, Dad. I really enjoy the day release course at college. I never would have thought I'd like being in a classroom.'

'Life is a lot like that; surprising twists and turns.'

'Tell me about it. Nicola's my other problem. I know her dreams are important to her, that she has to study hard for her exams to get to vet school, but it's just not working, Dad. She makes excuses not to see me; she always has more important things to do.

'I'm beginning to think I'm too young for all this hassle. Both of us want to go in different directions.

'It annoys me that her career has to come before everything else. She's going to be away for years at uni and, however much she denies it, I think I'm holding her back. We just don't seem to gel any more.'

Wow! His son really had grown up! Dan looked at him with admiration, knowing he had tough decisions to make, but knowing also that he would make the right choices. Sam was well on the way to becoming a man.

'Have you given any thought to what you might do next?'

Sam shrugged and exhaled slowly.

'I've got one or two ideas, but I don't think I want to talk about them yet.'

'Fair enough.'

'That's why I wanted to come here — to have a change of scene — get some space to sort my head out.'

'I'm glad you did. So is your mother. She worries about you.'

'Yeah. I know.' He met his father's steady gaze. 'I want to check things out first before I decide. Can we do this again, Dad?'

Wrapping an arm around Sam's shoulder, Dan drew his son close.

'Of course, lad, any time.'

'It Isn't Fair!'

'Hey, wait up, Laura!' Leaving school that Thursday, Laura hesitated on the pavement beside Fiona and turned in the direction of the voice calling her.

She waved when she saw her brother across the road.

'Who is that?' Fiona demanded, grinning as Sam dodged the traffic and came across to join them.

'Hi.' He thrust his hands deep in his pockets and fell into step beside them.

'Hi, Sam.' Laura smiled, sensing her friend jigging impatiently beside her. 'This is my friend, Fiona. Fiona, this is my brother, Sam.'

Fiona stepped forward with a cheeky grin, pushing her hair back to secure a good look at him.

'Grand to meet you, Sam.'

'Yeah, you, too.'

'So where's Laura been hiding you?'

'Fiona!' Laura giggled. Her friend really was incorrigible. 'I told you Sam had come home for a few days.'

Sam seemed dumbstruck, Laura thought, as they walked farther along the pavement. Fiona was chattering nineteen to the dozen, flirting outrageously

— and her brother looked as if he was enjoying it.

'So, what are you doing here?' Laura asked, reclaiming their attention.

Sam drew out the folded sheaf of paper tucked under his arm and waved it at Laura.

'I had stuff to do in town. I thought I'd walk back with you.'

'Oh. We were just waiting for Fiona's mum to see if I can go to her place.'

'Never mind then, I'll head on home.' He paused, smiling at Fiona. 'Hope to see you again some time.'

'Me, too,' Fiona breathed, her cheeks flushed.

Laura couldn't help laughing at her friend.

'You're shameless!'

'And your brother's hot! His eyes are just to die for.'

'For goodness' sake, Fiona, it's just Sam. Anyway, I thought you were sweet on Declan?'

Fiona shrugged, spinning round on the pavement in excitement.

'Not really. Declan's great and all that, but I'm just like a kid sister to him.'

'Right.'

Laura looked away, suddenly stunned at the rush of feeling which swamped her on learning her friend didn't fancy Declan after all. But why should that bother her? It wasn't as if she even liked boys.

'OK,' Fiona demanded, linking arms and snapping Laura from her reverie. 'So, give me the low-down. Does Sam have a girlfriend?'

'Yes. Her name's Nicola and she's studying to be a vet.'

'Rats.' Fiona's smile faded and she glanced along the road in the direction Sam had gone. 'But he's only sixteen, isn't he?' Squaring her shoulders as Laura nodded, Fiona's smile returned. 'Well then, all is not lost! Oh, here's Ma.'

She danced across the pavement as the Land-Rover pulled up and the door opened.

'I thought you'd forgotten me! Is it OK for Laura to come back?'

'I don't think that's a good idea at the moment,' Teresa declined stiffly, her face pinched and unfriendly.

'Ma!'

Laura stepped forward, an unaccustomed flash of anger burning inside her.

'It's all right, Fiona.' She smiled at her friend, then turned to face the woman who was upsetting her own mother.

'I'm sorry, Mrs Harrington. I know things are very difficult for you just now, but it isn't fair to blame my mother. She hasn't done anything wrong. And it isn't fair to take it out on me and my friendship with Fiona,' Laura protested, quietly but firmly, amazing herself with her temerity.

'We are all upset at what's happened, but Mum especially so, because you're supposed to be her friend.'

Teresa looked at the girl in astonishment, seeing her flushed cheeks, the tears welling up in her eyes. Before she had a chance to reply, Laura turned and ran in the direction of home.

★ ★ ★

How could she have done such a thing? Laura was absolutely mortified. Seeing Sam up ahead, she slowed down, fretting to herself. She had never spoken to anyone like that in her life, let alone an adult. But she had just been so infuriated thinking of her mother's distress, and the unfairness of it all. She and Fiona shouldn't be denied their friendship.

Turning the corner Sam glanced back and saw her. He waited for her to catch up.

'What's wrong?' He frowned at the sight of her tear-stained face.

'I've just been silly. It's nothing.'

'Out with it, Laura.'

'Fiona's mother is Mum's friend, Teresa Harrington. It's her dairy which is mixed up in this business with the hotel and the food poisoning scare.

She's been really off with Mum the last few days.

'Anyway, she said I'd better not spend time at the farm with Fiona any more and I lost my rag and said it wasn't fair, and that she was behaving badly. And she's the grown-up!'

'Wow!' Sam grinned, slipping his arm round her shoulders. 'It's not like you to lose your cool, Laura!'

A reluctant smile escaped.

'I shouldn't have said what I did, though, Sam.'

'Did you shout? Were you rude?'

'No.' She frowned. 'It wasn't like that. I just said it quietly. You know, like they tell you about making complaints in shops and stuff — keep calm.'

'Well, there you are then.' Her brother smiled. 'Nothing to worry about.'

'Mum will be mad, Sam.'

'I doubt it, Laura. She'll be pleased you stuck up for yourself. Anyway, your friend Fiona looks a feisty madam. I bet she speaks her mind.'

'Yes, she does.' Laura laughed, running on ahead. 'And she's taken a real shine to you!'

Apology

Sam chased after her and they were still laughing when they burst through the rear entrance to the kitchen. Looking harassed, their mother turned towards them, the telephone in one hand.

'She's just come in now, Teresa. Just a moment.' With a puzzled frown, she held out the phone. 'Laura, Fiona's mother wants a word with you.'

Her heart thumping against her ribs, Laura felt sick to her stomach. Sam gave her an encouraging pat on the head as he passed and she reluctantly stepped forward to take the phone.

'H-hello,' she stammered nervously.

'Laura, are you all right?'

'Yes, thank you, Mrs Harrington.'

There was a pause before Teresa spoke again.

'Look, love, I just wanted to say I'm sorry. You were right. It's wrong of me to take it out on you and Fiona — and your mum, come to that. You're welcome here at any time. I hope you'll come up and spend time with us this weekend.'

Her cheeks burning, Laura clutched the phone.

'I'd love to. And I'm sorry, too.'

'No need. Tell your ma I'll ring her in the morning when we have more time to talk. OK? Fiona will see you at school tomorrow.'

'OK . . . and thanks.'

'No, Laura. Thank you.'

Laura hung up, still feeling a bit shaky.

'What was all that about?' her mother asked, half pre-occupied with the evening preparations.

'Nothing, really. Mrs Harrington says she'll have a chat with you tomorrow and I can go up there at the weekend. I think she's over her huff!'

Delighted things had worked out,

and thrilled at the prospect of spending time at the stables with Fiona, Laura grabbed her bag and hurried upstairs to change. Her cheeks still flushed, she realised she would probably see Declan, too.

★   ★   ★

'How are you holding up?' Kathleen grimaced as she set two mugs of coffee down on the desk in the office. The tense lines by his eyes and mouth betrayed the fact that Dan's worries mirrored her own.

'It's frightening, not knowing what's going to happen.'

'I know.'

She watched as he picked up his mug and took a drink.

'Some of the guests have been a bit concerned. Have we had any more cancellations?'

'No, thank goodness. It helps that all the Dooleys are on the mend and no-one else has come down with it.'

Dan sighed, rubbing one hand around the back of his neck. His whole body felt tight and sore. 'I just wish we would hear something about the test results.'

'I didn't think it would take this long. They said three or four days, and it will be Friday tomorrow.'

'I'll ring the Environmental Health Officer in the morning,' he promised. 'Have things thawed out a bit with Teresa?'

Kathleen frowned.

'She is still upset. She's worried about her own business, naturally. I think Laura had a run-in with her this afternoon.'

'In what way?'

'I'm not sure, but Teresa was on the phone to speak to Laura when she came home from school. Laura looked much happier afterwards. She said she'd been invited up to spend time with Fiona at the weekend, and that Teresa would chat to me tomorrow. It sounds promising . . . but who knows?'

'Laura's improved a lot since we

came here,' Dan said proudly. 'So have the twins.'

Kathleen nodded her agreement, wrapping her hands around her mug.

'The thought of everything crashing down around us is too horrible to contemplate.'

'Don't start thinking that yet.'

'It's hard not to.'

'I know.' Hearing the quiver in her voice, Dan reached out to take her hand in his.

'All is not lost yet, love. I spoke with Ms O'Rourke at the bank earlier, to postpone our meeting with her until next week. She was very understanding and I think she's still interested in working with us.'

'That's one less worry then,' Kathleen agreed, managing a smile. 'It's a shame it had to be this week that Sam came. I'm going to miss him when he goes back. Has he said much to you?'

Dan hesitated, not sure how much Sam wanted him to reveal just yet.

'We've had a bit of a chat. He said he

had things to think about and would talk to me again before he left. He's growing up, Kath.'

'Yes.' Kathleen looked down at the table-top, her eyes stinging with unshed tears.

'It's hard to let go, isn't it?'

'Very.' Dan smiled.

Before he could offer any further comfort, the fax machine clattered into life as it churned out a message. Dan reached out to take the paper and noticed the heading — *URGENT*. His breath caught in his throat.

'What is it?' Kathleen demanded.

'Kath, the waiting is over. They know what's wrong with the Dooleys.'

The fate of the hotel and all their dreams was about to be decided . . .

8

Smitten

'Are you out here, Fiona?' Laura called as she entered the stable yard, fresh faced and excited at the prospect of the weekend ahead.

A movement off to one side caught her attention. Perhaps Fiona was saddling Molly, she thought, but it was Declan who she found in the stable brushing down one of the ponies.

'Oh!' Laura gasped.

'Hello, Laura.'

His voice was warm and friendly.

'Hi,' she murmured, hoping he couldn't see the flush blossoming on her cheeks.

'Fiona's running an errand for her da,' he explained. 'She shouldn't be long.'

Feeling awkward, Laura took a

couple of steps backwards.

'OK, thanks. I'm sorry to have bothered you.'

'You haven't. Why don't you come and sit down, and wait for her here?'

'Are you sure?'

Declan's dark eyes crinkled as he smiled at her.

'No problem. Just give me five minutes then I'll teach you how to clean tack.'

'OK, thanks. I'd like that.'

In the tack-room Laura settled nervously beside Declan, glancing at his handsome profile. The faint aromas of saddle-soap, leather and horse teased her nostrils. She watched as he took a bridle apart with practised expertise and laid the pieces out in front of them. He collected a couple of sponges, his fingers brushing against hers as he passed one to her.

Laura held her breath as she met his gaze.

'Um . . . I haven't cleaned tack before. What do I do?'

'Get a wee bit of water on the sponge

— not too much now. Grand. First, use it to wipe the dirt off the straps. Then smooth it along the bar of soap, that's right, and work it into the leather.' Declan demonstrated, watching her as she copied his movements.

'Like this?'

'Sure, you've got it already!'

They worked companionably for a while, but Laura felt strange — keenly aware of Declan's proximity.

'Don't you mind this job?' she asked after a moment. 'Fiona hates it.'

'I know she does! She's no patience, that girl. She doesn't know how to be quiet. I like cleaning tack, though. It's relaxing. It gives me time to think. Is it boring you?'

'No, of course not! I'm enjoying it.'

'Me, too.'

Something about his voice sent a shiver of awareness down her spine. Turning to face him, she met the intensity of his gaze and saw an expression she didn't recognise, but which sent a curl of excitement rippling through her. Flustered, she dropped her gaze and tried to concentrate on her task.

'So, how are things?' he asked after a short silence. 'I heard you'd had a few problems up at the hotel?'

'It's been horrible. Mum and Dad have had a hard time getting things going since we moved here. I was really frightened it would all go wrong, especially when the guests fell ill. It looked like food poisoning and they could have closed us down, you see.'

'What happened?'

'Well, just when things were really tense, waiting for the test results to come back, a fax arrived from America, from the relatives of the family staying with us,' Laura explained. Her eyes shone as she warmed to her theme, finding Declan easy to talk to.

'It turns out that they were all at some celebration dinner a day or two before they came to Ireland and that's where they picked up this bug.'

'Then it was nothing to do with your hotel at all — or the dairy?'

She met Declan's smile and beamed back at him.

'Exactly! Their relatives in America are all sick as well, and whatever the bug was, it takes several days to have any effect. So that's why they didn't fall ill until they were already with us.

'Now Mum's had the all-clear from the Environmental Health people. So has the dairy. My mum and Fiona's are finally speaking again. The Dooley family go home soon, but they've been very apologetic and say they'll come back for a proper holiday next summer — and recommend us to everyone in America!'

'That's brilliant, Laura.' Declan grinned. He shifted closer to her and slipped his arm around her shoulders to hug her.

'I Love It Here'

She allowed herself to rest against him for a moment, feeling a welter of conflicting emotions. Declan looked down at her, his eyes darkening. Suddenly, he brushed some wisps of hair back from her face and dropped a kiss on her cheek before letting her go and returning to his task.

'Your parents must be delighted.'

'Yes.' Laura struggled to find her voice. Her cheek tingled where his lips had brushed softly against it. She wanted to press her fingers to the spot but felt foolish in front of him. Instead, she cleared her throat and continued working.

'Yes, Mum and Dad are really chuffed. We all are. I love it here. I would hate it if things went wrong now and we had to move away.'

Again Declan's gaze sought hers.

'So would I,' he confided huskily.

Before she could respond, footsteps sounded in the yard outside.

'Laura?'

'In the tack-room,' Declan called.

'Whatever are you doing in here?' Fiona demanded with a laugh as she burst through the door, all energy and brimming with life. Podge, the rapidly growing puppy, trotted at her heels.

Laura stood up awkwardly.

'Declan was teaching me how to clean tack.'

'That's dead boring, Declan!' Fiona complained. 'Come on, Laura, it's time you had another riding lesson.'

As Fiona set about gathering the tack to get Molly ready for a ride, Laura smiled shyly at Declan. The pair followed Fiona out into the yard.

'Thanks, Declan,' Laura murmured, handing back the sponge.

'Sure, any time,' he replied, his tone sincere.

Fiona hurried out to the stables, oblivious to the atmosphere in the tack-room.

Laura walked to the door before hesitating.

'Bye.'

'See you, Laura.' Declan smiled at her before turning and going back inside to finish his work.

Laura hugged herself, unable to keep

the smile off her face.

With Podge bounding beside her, she went in search of Fiona. She really couldn't wait to see Declan again.

A Surprising Evening

Stephen felt ridiculously nervous as he pulled up outside the hostel that Saturday and climbed out of the car. Was he crazy, taking Annie out?

Things had been tempestuous between them from the first, and his break from the fiery Roisin at Easter still made him wary of further involvement.

It was nothing to get steamed up about, he told himself as Annie stepped out to meet him — just a meal and a drink.

She looked cool and fresh in jeans, boots and a fleecy top. Her short blonde hair shone with life and framed her face, the wispy fringe feathering her brow.

'Hi,' he said, trying not to stare. She

looked gorgeous. 'All set?'

With a brief nod, Annie rounded the car. Stephen frowned. Either she was regretting her decision to come out with him, or something had happened since he had last seen her.

'Are you OK, Annie?'

'Fine.' She slid him a wary glance and smiled stiffly. 'Where are we going?'

'I thought some food at Pat's and a cosy drink and a chat by the fire in Buckleys afterwards. Have you been there yet?'

'No, but everyone says I should. Am I dressed too casually for Pat's? Should I go and change?'

His gaze lingered on her, and when it reached her face, he saw a faint blush stain her cheeks.

'You look perfect,' he assured her, his voice husky.

Silence settled around them. A soft drizzle fell as he drove back towards town. The night sky was dark and starless, thanks to the clouds. Annie appeared to relax, but he couldn't banish the idea that something was wrong.

'Pat's and Buckleys are part of the same family business,' Stephen informed her as they drew up in the carpark. They walked along College Street to the restaurant. 'I booked a table.'

They were soon seated and being served by friendly staff, and Annie could see why the place had such a good reputation. She studied the menu, trying to put the day's upset from her mind, disturbed that Stephen had been intuitive enough to sense that something was wrong. She hoped he wasn't going to pursue it.

Once they'd both ordered local fish dishes, Annie sat back and fiddled with her napkin. She felt edgy and nervous.

She had been foolish to accept this invitation. Stephen Fitzgerald's effect on her was far too confusing for this to have been a sensible idea.

Aware of his steady blue gaze, Annie bit her lip.

'So,' Stephen began and Annie

tensed, expecting more questions about her mood. 'You promised to tell me all about Killarney Provincial Park in Canada.'

Annie's mouth curved in a relieved smile.

'I did.'

'We were talking before about the acid rain problems.'

'Indeed. Sudbury, in Ontario, has a long history of air pollution from mining and smelting, which began back in the 1880s. They put up the superstack chimney in 1972 but all it did was spread the emissions over a wider area. The acid rain fallout has affected the chemical balance of many of the lakes.'

She paused, wondering if she was talking too much, but Stephen was leaning forward, listening to her and apparently interested. Encouraged, she carried on.

'They found that even as far as the Killarney Provincial Park, water had been affected by sulphur dioxide. The park has always been an attraction for visitors and the loss of aquatic life was significant.'

'It must have impacted on the tourist trade,' Stephen commented.

'Of course. Many people's incomes depend on the visitors.' She broke off as their food was served and both were silent for a few moments as they enjoyed their fish. 'This is good.'

'And from local unpolluted waters!' Stephen's eyes twinkled. 'What did the authorities do about the pollution?'

Annie tucked some stray wisps of hair behind her ear and took a sip of mineral water. She told him about the liming programme and efforts to improve the water quality that some-how never achieved the desired results.

'Are things still bad?'

'The problems aren't as extreme now. Things are starting to improve, but it takes a long time. The park itself remains a beautiful piece of wilderness, though. You would love it, Stephen.'

She met his gaze, acknowledging what a good listener he was.

'Tell me more about the park itself. It's enormous, isn't it?'

'Your national park here in Ireland is — what — ten thousand hectares, at the most?'

Stephen nodded in agreement, forking up his final piece of fish.

'That's about it. What about Ontario?'

'Forty-eight-thousand, five hundred hectares.'

'Wow!'

They lingered over the remains of their meal and Annie chatted easily, telling him of all the different kinds of wildlife, the back country, the pine-covered mountains, the bogs and lakes and the whole gamut of breathtaking scenery that meant so much to her.

'It sounds an amazing place.' Stephen paid the bill and escorted her outside. 'I'd like to see it one day.'

'You'll have to ask for an exchange and come to study bear and bobcats and moose instead of red deer!'

'Maybe!' He laughed. 'Come on,' he said, linking his arm with hers. 'Buckleys is only two doors along.'

★   ★   ★

Annie discovered the oak-panelled bar was every bit as friendly and atmospheric as people claimed. Stephen found them a reasonably quiet corner by a turf fire and she could feel its heat as she sat down at the table.

Everyone seemed to know and like Stephen, she realised, watching as he was waylaid to and from the bar, chatting easily with both staff and customers alike. Perhaps she had misjudged him at first. Her break-up from Neil had coloured her emotions.

She frowned, remembering the letter she had received that day.

'You're doing it again.' Stephen joined her at the table.

'What?'

He set down her glass of wine and his half of Guinness and sat beside her.

'Looking troubled.'

Her expression closed and her gaze skittered away. Stephen reached out and took her hand in his, circling his thumb in her palm.

'Talk to me, Annie. Tell me what's wrong.'

She hesitated so long he thought she was going to ignore him, but at least she didn't pull her hand away. Finally she sighed and turned to face him, her grey eyes confused.

'I had a letter this morning from home . . . from Neil.'

A knot of disappointment tightened inside him. She was involved with someone? He should have known. He cleared his throat.

'Who's Neil?'

'My ex-fiancé. We didn't part on very good terms when I came over here.'

'I had no idea.' Maybe all was not lost, Stephen thought to himself. 'And what he said in this letter upset you?'

'He wants to discuss things, wants me to go back to Canada at Christmas and give up my 'foolish notions'.' She gave a harsh laugh, the fingers of her free hand playing with the stem of her glass. 'I've had more than enough time, apparently, to come to my senses.'

Stephen frowned.

'About what?'

'Him — and my career.'

'OK.' This was getting heavier than he had expected. 'That's what Neil wants. More importantly, Annie, what do you want?'

'I . . . ' She broke off and glanced self-consciously round the bar.

'Let's get out of here,' he suggested, sensing her discomfort.

'You don't mind?'

'No, of course not,' he fibbed, holding on to her hand as he guided her back outside.

'I am sorry,' she murmured as they walked back to the car. 'I've spoiled the evening.'

His fingers tightened reassuringly on hers.

'You haven't, Annie. We can come

back and you can experience Buckleys another time.'

'Thank you.' She smiled as he started the car and drove out of town, relieved to find that he wasn't giving her the brush-off.

'No problem.'

Hidden Depths

Silence settled between them, and before long he was drawing up outside the hostel. It was in darkness, the only light the one outside the main door. He'd thought she'd be off like a startled fawn again, but instead she sat with him and he switched off the engine, waiting.

'You asked what I wanted,' she said at last, her expression hidden by the shadows in the car. 'My work is important to me, I love what I do. I love the independence I've regained these last weeks. Neil . . . well, he's a successful lawyer. He's looking for a corporate wife, an accessory.

'I didn't notice at first that he was shaping me for the rôle. He was furious when I said I was taking this chance to come to Ireland. But I've studied hard, Stephen. I'm not prepared to give it all up for anyone — and certainly not for Neil.'

'And you shouldn't be expected to. If you did, you would only resent it further down the line.'

'You understand, don't you?'

Her tone betrayed her surprise and he nodded. For a moment Stephen wondered whether to tell her about Roisin, and the similar decision he had faced, but he held back, not wanting to alter the balance of the conversation.

His gaze sought hers in the dimness.

'And do you want to go home to Neil?'

A shiver ran through her at the tone of his question.

'No.' She swallowed, sensing he was asking more than it appeared on the surface. 'No, I don't want Neil any more.'

Stephen's hand reached out, his fingers trailing her cheek. Unconsciously, she caught her breath as he leaned towards her, his mouth gently seeking hers, moving firmly against her as she instinctively kissed him back.

Too soon, he was pulling away. Aware she was clinging to him, Annie dropped her hands, confused and unsettled by what had happened. She gathered herself together and opened the door.

'Thanks for this evening . . . for listening.'

'My pleasure, Annie. Goodnight.'

'Night, Stephen.'

She closed the door and walked reluctantly towards the hostel, hesitating as he started the car and drove away.

There were depths to Stephen Fitzgerald. It had been a surprising evening all round, she decided, letting herself in. As she readied herself for bed, Neil was the last person on her mind.

A Fond Farewell

'Why do we have to get up this early on a Sunday, Mum?' James yawned widely.

In the other bunk, Luke settled down again, but Kathleen pulled the duvet off.

'Mum!' he complained.

'Come on now, boys.' She chivvied her drowsy children. 'You know your brother leaves early this morning. We're having a family breakfast to see him off.'

'It's the middle of the night!'

'Don't be daft, James. I don't have time to mess about. Get up, please, both of you, and come down to the kitchen. Quietly!'

Luke was already struggling into his trousers and sweatshirt, but James lingered.

'Can I keep my jammies on so I can

come back to bed when Sam's gone?'

'If you must. Just get on with it, please.'

Kathleen shook her head and hurried back to the kitchen. Laura was already there, dressed in her riding clothes.

'You're up bright and early.' Kathleen smiled, continuing her preparations for their early breakfast.

'I thought I'd make the most of it and go up to the stables. Would you like me to set the table?'

'That would be great, love. Thank you.'

Sam's visit had rushed by. Kathleen bit her lip and kept working, anything to banish the sadness of having to say goodbye to her eldest son once again. She stifled her tender feelings as he came into the kitchen, tousled and half asleep.

'All right, love?' She took the opportunity to give him a quick hug and kiss. 'You always hated early starts.'

'I still do!'

Kathleen smiled as he helped Laura

carry things through to the family dining-room. Dan was already up, she discovered as he came into the kitchen. He moved stiffly. Kathleen opened her mouth to speak, then quickly closed it again. He hated it when she fussed over him.

'Anything I can do?' he asked.

'No. We're just about ready. Perhaps you could hurry the twins up.'

'Sure.'

Before long they were all sitting round the table tucking into a rare breakfast together.

'It's been so good having you here, Sam.'

'I've had a great time, Mum. It's been cool.' He grinned round the table at them. 'Who'd have thought James would actually like school!'

James made a face, hungrily spooning in his cereal, dribbling milk down the front of his pyjamas.

'Not me,' he admitted, making them all laugh.

'I love it here, especially when I get to

go to the park with Uncle Stephen,' Luke chipped in.

Sam ruffled Luke's hair.

'That's great. Do you still want to be a ranger one day?'

'You bet!'

Spreading some honey on his toast, Sam shot a glance at his sister.

'You're looking wicked, Laura.'

'Leave off,' she protested, flushing with embarrassment.

'It's true,' Sam insisted. 'You've changed since I last saw you. You've really come out of yourself. Hasn't she, Dad?'

'Absolutely.' Dan nodded and everyone agreed, making Laura blush even more.

'I think being friends with Fiona has done wonders for you.' Kathleen smiled. 'She's very bubbly.'

'She certainly seems like a livewire.' Sam grinned. He wouldn't have minded seeing more of his sister's friend.

All too soon it was time to make a move, and Dan went out to bring the car round. Forcing a wide smile, Sam hugged the twins and Laura, then walked with his mother to the door. Dawn was breaking, and the trees and hills were silhouetted against the sky.

'Give my love to Gran and Grandpa.'

'Don't worry, love, I will. And you'll come and visit again soon, won't you?'

Sam swallowed the lump in his throat at the emotion in his mother's voice.

'I'll definitely be home for Christmas.'

He allowed her to envelop him in a desperate hug. Closing his eyes, he held her back, prolonging the moment together as long as he could.

'Come on, Mum,' he teased. 'You'll be late with the guests' breakfasts at this rate!'

'Well, they'll just have to wait for once!'

'Mother! I never thought I'd see the day!'

'Get on with you, now.' Kissing him again, she stood back. 'Take care, love.'

'I will, and you.'

He ran down the steps and jumped in the car. It was a wrench to leave this place.

'OK?' Dan asked.

'Yeah, let's go.'

But before they had travelled more than a few yards down the driveway, another car turned in, blocking their way.

'It's Uncle Stephen!' Sam lowered his window as Stephen's car drew alongside.

'I'm glad I caught you. I wanted to say goodbye,' Stephen said, much too cheerily for the early hour. 'Have a good trip, Sam.'

They headed out of Killarney on the Tralee road. Sam was thankful it was only a fifteen-minute drive to the airport. He hated goodbyes and felt even more wretched the closer they came to their destination.

'Thanks, Dad.'

'What for?'

'Everything. For not pressuring me.

I'm waiting for some more information before I make a decision.'

'I'll be here when you're ready, Sam.'

Sam was proud of the new understanding between them.

'Can I ask you something?' They were approaching Kerry Airport and he had to have the answer to one very important question before he left.

'Of course.'

'Do you miss it? The fire service, I mean.'

His dad hesitated and shifted uncomfortably behind the wheel.

'Every day, Sam. Every day,' he finally admitted.

Sam's stomach tightened at the sadness in his father's smile.

'I'm sorry.'

'Don't be. It was a wonderful life. If I had the time over I'd do it all again.'

'Does it upset you to talk about it?'

'No, not really. I'm proud of the service and all those in it. Proud to have been a part of it. It's like a second family — I miss the camaraderie with the crew the most.' He pulled over near the terminal building. 'It's a great life. I'd recommend it to anyone.'

Sam stared ahead, lost in thought, then jumped as his dad patted his shoulder.

'You'd best get on and check in.'

Sam fixed a broad smile on his face and hugged his father awkwardly.

'Don't get out, Dad. I'll be OK.'

'Are you sure?'

'Absolutely.' No way was he going to let his dad walk all through the terminal and hang around for ages in discomfort. 'Good luck with the woman from the bank. I hope you finish the website!'

'I'll let you know how things go. Take care of yourself, son, and remember that your mum and I will support whatever you want to do.'

'Thanks. I'm going to miss you all. Love you, Dad.'

Sam hurried off before his resolve broke, before he embarrassed himself by showing his emotions.

By Christmas he intended to have finalised his plans.

A Waiting Game

'Your ideas are very interesting,' Shelagh O'Rourke mused. She gave little away as she accepted the cup of tea Kathleen had provided. 'Thank you, Mrs Jackson. I would say your plans are ambitious, but interesting.'

It had been a long afternoon. Kathleen sneaked a covert glance at her watch, thankful that her parents were keeping the twins for a while after school. Laura was at Fiona's. All she had to worry about were the preparations for the guests' dinner, but when she had popped into the kitchen to make the tea, Josie had seemed to have everything under control.

Dan could not have expected this visit to go on so long. Kathleen certainly hadn't. But Ms O'Rourke was nothing if not thorough. She had inspected every nook and cranny of the hotel, dissected their ideas for the renovations, pored over their business plan, pondered their financial situation, and questioned them endlessly.

As she handed a cup of tea to Dan, Kathleen noted the drawn lines around his mouth that indicated his tension and his discomfort. This appointment had run on so long he'd missed his medication. Surreptitiously, she slipped a couple of pills into his hand and slid the plate of biscuits across the desk, earning herself a tired smile as he mouthed his thanks.

Kathleen sat down with her own tea, and endeavoured to maintain her composure as Ms O'Rourke frowned over the papers in her lap. Ms O'Rourke's raven hair was drawn back in a severe but impeccable plait. Her green eyes were sharp and intelligent, and despite her youth she gave the impression of confidence and efficiency.

Hurdles

'The hotel is obviously showing its age following your parents' years here, Mrs Jackson.'

The green gaze swept over her and Kathleen managed a nervous smile.

'But they built up an excellent reputation,' Dan interjected. 'A reputation I believe we can capitalise on if we're able to carry out the renovations.'

Shelagh O'Rourke's mouth pouted in consideration.

'True, the refurbishments are sensible ones and necessary to bring the hotel into the twenty-first century.'

'There is no reason to believe that tourism will be any less viable in Killarney now than it was last century,' Kathleen was moved to point out, stung by the woman's criticisms. If only she would make a decision one way or another!

Once more Shelagh O'Rourke's intimidating gaze swung between them.

'Both of you are inexperienced in

271

hotel management.' Her cool smile was noncommittal.

'I am,' Dan agreed, quiet determination evident in his tone. 'But Kathleen grew up here, learning the business from her parents until her late teens.'

'Granted. You've displayed incredible enthusiasm and drive.'

Kathleen exchanged a glance with Dan as the bank's business manager once more flicked through papers. They seemed to be lurching from one nerve-wracking moment to another these last weeks. As each hurdle was overcome, another uncertainty rose up to challenge them, threatening their very future in Ireland.

Dan was right; they did need to carry out this refurbishment if the hotel was to move forward. But to do that, they needed extra backing from the bank. This woman was their last chance. Would she give them that break?

'One other thing you need to consider,' Ms O'Rourke continued, seemingly intent on putting more obstacles in their way, 'is what direction you wish to go in.'

'In what way?' Dan frowned.

'Do you plan to completely remodernise and become more trendy, catering for a younger market?'

'No!'

Kathleen's response was adamant, but she stilled her annoyance as Dan shook his head.

'My wife is right, Ms O'Rourke. We have done a considerable amount of research with past, present and future guests, discussing their needs and requirements and finding out what attracts them here. We've also studied some of the other hotels in the area.

'Our conclusions are that we should capitalise on our strengths and traditions — our homely, warm, welcoming family feel. It makes more sense to rework what we do best, rather than set off in an entirely unfamiliar direction.'

'I see!' One neat eyebrow raised and a small smile curved the thin line of her mouth. 'You seem to have done your homework, Mr Jackson.'

'Yes, we have. The opinions, needs and comfort of our guests are of primary importance. We take them very seriously, Ms O'Rourke,' Dan replied, an edge of steel underlying his calm tones.

'We're not playing at this. Our plans are to close during December and January. We have been assured by various contractors who have given us quotes that the work can be completed in that time, but it will, of course, mean two months with no income.

'However, with the website up and running, a push for publicity and a fully refurbished hotel, we anticipate improvements in bookings and income from next year onwards.'

With a cool and graceful nod of her head, Shelagh O'Rourke rose to her feet and shook hands.

'Thank you, both. It has been an informative afternoon.'

'We appreciate your coming to see us, Ms O'Rourke.' Dan smiled, rounding the desk to show her out.

Kathleen opened her mouth to make further queries, but Dan took her hand in his and squeezed her fingers in warning, silencing her. Disappointed and on edge, she bit back her words, walking beside him as they escorted their visitor down the wide hallway.

Shelagh O'Rourke turned on the steps to bestow a final cool smile.

'I'll report back to my superior and contact you in due course.'

'If you need any further information . . .'

'Like I say, I'll be in touch.' She countered Dan's comment dismissively. 'Good afternoon, Mr Jackson, Mrs Jackson.'

Kathleen leaned against Dan as they watched her take her leave.

'I didn't like her, Dan.'

'We don't have to like her. The question is whether she approves our business plan or not and loans us the money.'

'She didn't give much away, did she?'

'No.' Dan walked back to the office,

sighing as he sat uncomfortably in his cushioned chair, his back aching.

'No, she didn't.'

'We should have asked what she thought,' Kathleen persisted, wrapping her arms around herself, seeking some kind of comfort.

'Which was just what she wanted us to do. We need to play it cool, Kath. If we had pressured her and appeared anxious, it may have indicated we were unprofessional or lacking confidence in our own abilities.'

She watched as he ran his hands through his hair.

'I suppose you're right. It just feels as if we are balancing on the edge all the time. If Ms O'Rourke turns us down, what then?'

'I don't know.' The expression in his eyes reflected his tiredness and concern. 'We can only take things step by step and do our best.'

'And in the meantime other people play games with our dreams.'

'Then let's hope Ms O'Rourke is a

competent competitor. There is nothing we can do now but wait — and hope she comes through for us.'

'And if she doesn't?'

'Then we'll have to make some very tough decisions.'

9

Invitation

'Well, that's the boys in bed at last.'

Laura glanced up as her mother came down the back stairs and into the kitchen, looking pale and harassed.

'Can I do anything to help, Mum?'

'Thank you, love, no. You finish your homework. I just have the tables to lay for the guests' breakfasts.' Kathleen hesitated, turning back to the table. 'Do you want more coffee, Dan?'

'I'm all right, thanks.'

Concerned at the tension simmering between her parents, Laura sighed and tried to concentrate on her maths as her mother disappeared in the direction of the hotel dining-room. Her father was sitting across from her at the kitchen table, reading the local paper.

Her homework completed, Laura

glanced up from her books and noted her father's sombre expression, and the lines of pain etched around his mouth. How bad were things, she worried? What would happen if they were unable to go ahead with refurbishing the hotel? There had been no news since that woman from the bank had called the week before.

She was so happy here — she liked it so much better than England. She was inwardly terrified that everything would go wrong and they would have to leave Killarney.

The telephone rang, making her jump. To save her father any discomfort, Laura rose swiftly to her feet.

'I'll get it.'

'Thanks, sweetheart.' Dan smiled.

Laura crossed to the kitchen extension and lifted the receiver.

'Good evening, Waterside Hotel.'

'Hi, Laura, it's Declan.'

His familiar voice made her tingle all over.

'Hello,' she replied, unable to believe

he was ringing her.

'I hope it's not too late to call.'

'No, it's fine.' Heat stained her cheeks as she met her father's questioning gaze.

'OK.' She could hear the smile in Declan's voice. 'Are you busy at the weekend?'

Her heart thudding, Laura tried to get her brain in gear.

'I'd just planned on going up to the stables as usual. Why?'

'I'm competing in an indoor competition in County Cork on Sunday. It's only a half-hour drive away. Fiona and her dad are coming, and I'd really like it if you joined us, Laura.'

'You would?' She stifled a groan. Couldn't she say anything sensible? 'Thank you, I'd love to.'

'Great!'

Again she met her dad's gaze, and she smiled shyly.

'I'll have to ask, but it should be OK.'

'Would you like me to talk to your parents?'

'No, thanks, I can do it. I'll let Fiona know at school tomorrow morning, shall I?'

'Or you could ring me yourself.'

Excitement flickered through her.

'Do you want me to?'

'Yes. I'd like that very much, Laura. About this time?'

'OK.'

She wrote down the number he gave her for the cottage, her pulse racing. There was silence for a moment and she held her breath, not wanting him to say goodbye yet.

'I'm counting on you to bring me luck on Sunday,' he confided, his voice dropping to a soft huskiness, which made Laura flutter with delight.

'I'll try,' she promised, curling the phone cord round her finger. 'Are you going to be riding Paprika?'

'No, he's too young and inexperienced at the moment for this kind of competition. I'm hoping to bring him out next year in the six and seven-year-old class,' Declan explained.

'I'll be riding an older horse of Jack's called Black Diamond. I've been competing on him this season.'

Her mother had come back into the kitchen. Aware that both her parents were watching her curiously, Laura's awkwardness returned.

'I'll look forward to Sunday.'

'Do you have to go now? Is someone else there?'

'Yes,' she admitted, feeling furtive even though she wasn't doing anything wrong.

'OK. But you'll ring me tomorrow?'

'I will. And thank you very much for asking me.'

'It wouldn't be the same without you there. I'll see you soon. 'Night, Laura.'

'Goodnight.'

She replaced the receiver reluctantly and, schooling her expression, turned round and returned to the table.

'Was that someone from school?' her mother asked.

'Mmmm, no,' Laura murmured, her gaze clashing with her father's and skittering away.

'No, it was about the weekend. Fiona and her dad are going to watch Declan compete at an indoor show-jumping thing on Sunday and I've been asked along as well. It's OK if I go, isn't it?'

'I don't see why not, Kath, do you?'

Laura met her dad's gaze, happy he had agreed without an inquisition. He smiled and sent her a conspiratorial wink that made her blush. Did he know? Had he guessed who she'd been talking to?

Sliding the piece of paper with Declan's number inside her maths text book, she began to pack up her things.

'Well,' her mother intervened, 'if Jack and Fiona are going I suppose it's fine. Where is it?'

'About half an hour away. Towards Cork,' Laura replied.

'And was that Fiona on the phone?'

'No.' Laura watched as her mother bustled round the kitchen getting things ready for the morning. 'Declan, actually.'

Her mother turned and stared at her in surprise.

'Oh! That was Declan asking you?'

'Yes.' Laura's chin rose defiantly and she sent a pleading look towards her father. 'Is that a problem?'

'Of course not, sweetheart.' Dan smiled, folding the paper and shifting in his chair.

Her mother frowned.

'But . . . '

'Is your homework finished?' her dad interrupted and Laura nodded. 'You get off to bed then.'

Laura rose thankfully to her feet and collected up her books. She gave her mum a hasty kiss and then rounded the table to her father's side.

''Night, Dad.'

'Sweet dreams,' he whispered, as she leaned down to hug him.

Smiling, her cheeks pink, Laura headed for the stairs, lingering out of sight as she heard her mother's protest.

'Dan! Exactly what was that all about, please?'

'It's nothing to get upset over, Kathleen,' he chided his wife.

'Laura's too young to have boys ringing her up!'

'She'll be fifteen in the New Year — and it's a harmless daytime outing. There will be plenty of people around.'

'But . . .'

Laura heard a chair scrape on the floor as her father stood up, and although his voice was quiet there was a thread of impatience in it when he spoke again.

'Don't spoil things for her, Kath. She deserves to have some fun, and the future is precarious enough at the moment. If it makes you feel better, I'll have a quiet word with Jack.'

'Well, all right.'

Her mother didn't sound happy, but at least they weren't arguing any more. Careful not to make a sound, Laura tiptoed away up the stairs, mortified at the thought of her dad speaking to Mr

Harrington about it. Whatever would Declan think of that?

Still, she told herself as she changed for bed and slid under the duvet, Declan had phoned her and asked her to watch him compete! It wasn't a date or anything, but he wanted her to be there.

Smiling, warm and happy, she closed her eyes and wished for Sunday to hurry up and arrive.

Heart To Heart

Back in his bedsit after work on Friday, nearly two weeks following his return from Ireland, Sam looked over the information that had arrived in the post. He was both excited and nervous. Now, he had all he needed to put his plans for his future into action.

The church bells down the road chimed the hour — six o'clock. He'd arranged to meet Nicola at seven. With a sigh, he put the papers back inside the envelope and went through to the tiny bathroom to wash and change. A little later, he pocketed his wallet and left the building.

This would be the first time he had seen Nicola since he had been to Ireland as she had cancelled their plans the weekend before. It was time they had a chat about where their relationship was going.

The November night was dry but cold. They'd arranged to meet at their favourite pizza restaurant, but as usual Nicola was late. Shrugging off his parka, Sam sat inside and nibbled a breadstick while he waited, his mind burdened.

'Have you been here long?' Nicola asked when she arrived ten minutes later.

Sam dropped a polite kiss on her cheek and shrugged.

'A while.'

'Oh! Sorry.' Her apology was mixed with surprise at his restrained manner. Smiling uncertainly, she sat down.

'Are you OK?'

'Yes. I'm good, thanks. You?'

'Yes, fine. Very busy. How was Ireland?'

He paused to allow the waiter to take their order before replying.

'It was great.'

'Are things going well?'

'They've had a few teething problems with the hotel, but they'll turn things round.'

'What about Laura and the twins?' Nicola asked politely.

'They're happy and settled.'

The food arrived and both were silent as they began to eat. Sam realised he could no longer ignore the awkwardness between them. Although Nicola gave the impression of being interested, she had made little effort to get in touch with him, or to see him since his return from Ireland. He often felt she wasn't really with him, even when they were together. Her mind was always somewhere else.

'It's not working, is it, Nic?' he asked softly after a while.

Her eyes widened.

'What? I . . . '

'Are you seeing someone else?'

'Sam!'

Her protest seemed more embarrassed than genuine as a light flush pinked her cheeks.

'Are you?' he repeated.

'Sort of. I don't know.' She stumbled over her answer as her eyes shimmered with tears. 'Not properly.'

'But you want to.' It was a statement, not a question, his emotions under more control than he'd expected.

'I think so.' Her hand trembled and she roughly brushed away an escaped tear. 'I'm sorry, Sam.'

He shook his head, a sad smile playing about his mouth.

'It's all right. We can't go on just for the sake of it, Nicola. It isn't fair to either of us.'

'I do care about you.'

'I know. And I care about you, too. But we've grown too far apart these last months.'

Nicola's eyes were dark with emotion as she twirled some strands of hair nervously round her fingers.

'What about you? Are you seeing anyone else, Sam?'

'No.' He leaned back in his chair and watched her. 'No, I'm not. But my plans have changed. You have years of hard work ahead of you with exams and training, and your dreams for the future are important. But I think we both know they don't include me.'

'So what are you going to do?'

'I'm going to Ireland to spend Christmas with the family. I don't think I'll be coming back, Nic.'

They left the restaurant and walked the dark, quiet streets to her house.

'I'll never forget you, Sam,' she whispered when they halted outside the gate.

'We had some good times.'

'Yes.'

He cupped her face in his hands and brushed a kiss across her cool lips.

'I wish you all the best, Nicola. I

hope your dreams come true.'

'Thanks.' She smiled through her tears. 'Good luck, Sam. Be happy.'

Good Fun

His steps brisk, Sam headed back to the bedsit. The evening had been a sad one, but the strongest emotion he felt now was relief. Nicola had been his first love, but they had grown apart and it was better they ended it now, while they were still friends.

Indoors, he opened the envelope that had arrived that day and looked again at the contents. Following his meeting in Ireland, and backed by a recommendation from the tutor on his day-release course at college, he was now being offered a place doing mechanical engineering in Killarney.

Picking up a pen, he carefully filled out the attached forms, signed them, and put them neatly in the return envelope. His task completed, his thoughts turned to Christmas, only seven weeks away . . . and to the secret he couldn't wait to share.

They would be pleased, he was sure, to have him home. But how would they react when they learned of his long-term plans to follow in his Dad's footsteps and join the fire service?

★ ★ ★

Annie felt ridiculously self-conscious, walking into Buckley's Bar on her own on Saturday evening. Despite it being a cold, wet November night, the place was buzzing. She resisted the urge to walk straight out again and headed towards the bar, smiling at the young woman who welcomed her.

'It's some evening, isn't it?' The barmaid grinned. 'What can I get you?'

'A glass of red wine, please.'

'Sure. Coming right up.'

As she waited, Annie glanced round, looking for familiar faces. Not that she had come here hoping to see Stephen, she scolded herself, a small frown of confusion puckering the smoothness of her brow. The atmosphere between them had thawed since their evening out. She realised now his friendly warmth was natural and she had taken to his easy-going manner. Stephen was good at his job and genuinely interested in hers. That was a new experience for Annie, after Neil's continual put-downs.

But Stephen had made no further invitation, and although Annie wasn't looking for any kind of attachment, she admitted she had felt disappointed.

'Can I get you anything else?' the barmaid asked, setting the glass of wine on the counter-top and reclaiming Annie's attention.

'No, thanks.' She searched in her purse for the money, still getting to grips with the unfamiliar euros. 'Is that OK?'

'Grand! Are you visiting family?' the friendly woman enquired, handing over the change.

Annie slipped the coins in her purse

and shook her head.

'No, I'm here for a year, working in the national park.'

'Ah, great! Some of the rangers are in tonight if you feel like company.' The woman pointed across the bar.

'Thanks, I might wander over.'

'Sure, they're a nice crowd, it'll be a good *craic*. My name's Jess, by the way.'

'I'm Annie.'

'Hope to see you again.'

As Jess moved away to serve other customers, Annie sipped her wine. Shouldering her bag, she wandered through the bar, wondering who was in from the park and whether it would be OK to go and join them. She hesitated, looking round.

Her breath caught in her throat as her gaze met Stephen's. He was sitting near the fire laughing with the other park staff but rose with a smile when he saw her, and gestured to her to join them.

Shyness gripped her as she threaded her way to the table, but the rest of the company greeted her with genuine welcome and shuffled round to make room for her. Within moments Annie found herself divested of her wet coat and squashed up on the seat next to Stephen.

'Hi.' His eyes crinkled at the corners as he smiled. 'It's good to have you join us.'

A knot of awareness tightening her stomach, Annie smiled back.

'Thanks.'

The evening passed quickly and she was glad she had come. The others included her in their chat, sharing stories and making her feel as if she belonged. Warmed by both the peat fire and the company, Annie relaxed. When people began to drift away she was surprised to find herself outside . . . and alone . . . with Stephen.

'My stomach thinks my throat's been cut!' he joked. 'Are you hungry?'

Annie laughed.

'Now you mention it, I am.'

'Come on then.' He took her hand in

his and led her down the street. 'What we need is a visit to Mike's.'

'Mike's?'

'On Plunkett Street. There's nowhere better for curry chips on a Saturday night!'

Somewhat uncertain, Annie nevertheless walked contentedly beside him. It felt like the most natural thing in the world, strolling along, hand in hand.

'Don't Take This The Wrong Way'

They soon arrived at Mike's and she was amazed to find the place so crowded.

'Looks like we've hit the folk heading home from tonight's concert. Do you want to wait here?' Stephen suggested, saving her from the good-natured scrum.

Annie watched as Stephen joined the queue. Sheltered though she was inside the doorway, she pulled her jacket tighter round her as it began to drizzle.

Before long Stephen was back with their orders.

'You OK?'

'My mouth is watering,' she admitted, her tastebuds stirring with the gorgeous tang of the food. 'I hadn't realised how hungry I was.' Nor, she thought, had she realised what good fun Stephen was.

'Let's get out of this weather.'

She matched his stride as he headed along the pavement and ushered her across the High Street.

'Where are we going?'

'It's not far to my house.'

'Oh, right.'

As they strolled along in companionable silence, Annie knew that the weight that had rested on her shoulders had finally lifted.

The rain intensified and they hastened along. She realised she was curious to see Stephen's home. She knew very little about his private life. She didn't even know if he had a girlfriend.

Her frown returned. Surely he wouldn't be taking her back to his house now, if he was involved with anyone else? Would he?

'We're here,' Stephen said as they turned up a short, paved driveway towards an attractive, two-storey, semi-detached house. It had a black slate roof and its walls were painted white on the upper floor with dark red brick below.

As Stephen shouldered open the front door and went ahead switching on lights, Annie followed, surprised at the homely warmth.

'Make yourself at home.' He showed her into the living-room. 'I'll get some plates.'

As he disappeared into the kitchen, Annie took off her coat and looked around. The room was bright and airy, decorated in pale yellows and blues, with a stripped pine floor, comfy furniture and a couple of local landscape paintings on the walls. The alcoves either side of the fireplace were lined with shelves full of books.

On the wooden mantelpiece over a

cast-iron open fire were a series of framed family photos. She looked at them more closely, recognising his parents and one of his twin nephews, Luke, who sometimes visited the park with him.

'All set.'

She spun round at the sound of his voice, embarrassed to have been caught snooping.

'Do you want to sit at the table or here by the fire?' he asked.

'By the fire would be lovely.'

Stephen gestured for her to sit down and handed her a plate. After banking up the fire, stirring the embers to life, he joined her on the sofa.

'Tuck in.' He smiled.

She hadn't expected the curry chips to be so tasty.

'They're really good.'

'Surprised?'

'Very,' she admitted, and his eyes crinkled with amusement, sparking her own in return. 'OK — so I had reservations!'

They enjoyed their impromptu meal in companionable silence, then Stephen cleared away the plates and made some coffee.

'You have a lovely home.' She smiled at him as he handed her a mug.

'Thank you.'

'Have you lived here long?'

'It was a wreck when I bought it five years ago,' he told her, retaking his place beside her and stretching out his long, denim-clad legs. 'It's been very satisfying bringing it back to life.'

'You did all this yourself?' Her surprise brought a grin to his face.

'All except the electrical stuff. I really enjoyed it.'

She sipped her coffee, enjoying the warmth.

'You've made it really cosy.'

'Better than the hostel, anyway.' He smiled.

'It's not so bad.'

'Aren't you finding it lonely out there with the season over?'

Annie gave what she hoped was a

nonchalant shrug.

'I'll get used to it.'

'But why, when you don't have to?'

'What do you mean?'

Stephen set his cup down and turned to face her.

'Annie, I don't want you to take this the wrong way, but I'm sure it isn't much fun out there and it'll be worse as the winter goes on. So . . . '

'So?' she prompted as his words trailed off, suddenly wary of where this was leading.

'I have masses more room than I can use.' His blue gaze, clear but intense, held hers.

'You'd be very welcome — if you'd care to move in here.'

'I'm Just So Happy!'

'This is amazing!' Laura exclaimed, her eyes wide with excitement.

She had never expected the venue to be so huge! The indoor arena had been

301

built to international size and specification, with banks of seating for the spectators.

Declan had performed brilliantly in the first part of the competition, guiding the large and spirited black horse round the course and ending with a clear round. It had been fantastic watching him. Laura put a hand to her throat, conscious of her pulse still racing. She couldn't wait for the jump-off to come!

'It's grand, isn't it?' Fiona grinned. 'Shall we go and look at the horses?'

'Can we?'

'Sure, aren't we part of Declan's team?'

Laura felt herself start to blush just at the mention of his name and she dipped her head in an attempt to hide her expression. Any disappointment she felt at scarcely seeing him today was tempered by her pleasure at being here — and the news that had arrived yesterday.

'You're away with the fairies, Laura!'

Surprised at Fiona's teasing, she stopped and stared at her friend.

'What?'

'Did you hear anything I said?'

'Sorry.' She spun round in the autumn sunshine, unable to contain her happiness.

'Oh, Fiona, I'm just so happy!'

Fiona laughed and hugged her.

'I wish you could have seen Mum and Dad's faces when the letter came yesterday! It's the best possible news. Now the bank are going to back us I don't have to be scared that we'll have to move back to England.'

'Your ma looked fit to burst when she dropped you off earlier!' Fiona grinned.

'I'm so pleased for them, Fi, they've worked so hard. It's time something went right. And the best thing is that we get to stay here!'

Arm in arm, they walked to the stable complex used by the competitors for their horses. They found Jack leaning on the door talking to Declan, who was inside attending to Black Diamond.

'Declan, we'll work on that tricky turn for the jump-off.' He broke off as they approached.

'There you are, girls.'

'Hi, Da.'

Laura watched as Jack ruffled his daughter's hair and then turned with a smile.

'And how are you enjoying your first indoor competition, Laura?'

'It was great, Mr Harrington. I thought Black Diamond and Declan were brilliant!'

His eyes twinkled.

'I'm not sure I'd go that far, but they did a good job.'

Laura silently insisted they were far better than good.

'Do you think they can win?' she asked, peering over the door at the large black horse inside, the white blaze running down his face.

'They have a good chance if they hold things together. Did Fiona explain the scoring? Do you know that in Declan's class these points count towards qualification?'

'No,' Laura answered uncertainly. Fiona had wandered on down the line of stables to look at the other horses. 'What do they qualify for?'

Jack turned and leaned his back against the door.

'If Declan wins today he'll qualify to ride in the Grand Prix final at the Belfast International next month.'

'Wow!'

A Tannoy announcement alerted the riders that a class was ending and Declan's jump-off was not too far away. The flurry of activity around the stables increased.

'Right, Declan, let's be getting on and warming up,' Jack instructed. 'I'll meet you in the exercise area. Laura, you'd best join up with Fiona and retake your seats. We'll meet you back at the lorry after the competition.'

'OK, Mr Harrington.'

Laura watched as he strode away towards the impressive arena and then looked round for Fiona. Behind her, the stable door opened and she felt a hand on her shoulder. She spun round and met Declan's enigmatic gaze.

'Hi.' She smiled shyly.

He took her hand and drew her just inside the stable door.

'Are you going to wish me luck?' Declan teased, pulling on his crash hat.

'Of course. I so hope you win.'

'Thanks.' Standing between her and Black Diamond, he leaned forward and touched a finger to his cheek. 'Go on, then.'

'Sorry?'

'My good luck kiss.'

Laura felt her cheeks flush.

'Oh!' Taking a deep breath, she moved nearer and pressed her lips to the smooth warmth of his face.

She stepped back, her lips tingling. Before either of them could speak, Fiona bounded up and opened the door.

'All set?' she asked. 'Come on, Laura, we'd best get back. Go for it, Declan!'

Her wits still scattered, Laura soon

found herself sitting next to Fiona in the arena waiting for the final part of the competition to start. She felt knotted up with nerves as the minutes ticked by, hardly hearing as Fiona chattered on.

There were nine horses in the jump-off and Declan was going second last. Laura wasn't sure she could stand the tension. Then the crowd was clapping as the commentator announced the arrival of the first competitor, who rode into the ring on a flighty grey horse.

'They'll never go clear,' Fiona whispered in Laura's ear. 'That horse is fast but careless.'

Sure enough, although the time appeared good, the rider making far tighter turns than Laura thought possible, the pair finished with two fences down. The next rider did a clear round, but it was slow. As each partnership came and went, Laura felt sick with anxious excitement.

By the time Declan rode into the

arena, looking magnificent on his beautifully turned out horse, there had been three clear rounds, and four riders with various faults.

Instinctively, Laura gripped Fiona's arm.

'This is it! Come on, let them win,' she murmured fervently.

Her heart was in her mouth as Declan took a final look round the shortened course, with its tight turns and tricky combinations.

Effortlessly, Black Diamond broke into a canter. Declan turned him in a graceful circle and passed through the timing beam.

Laura felt herself move in rhythm with the horse's stride as she watched Declan take the first fence with ease. Black Diamond obeyed every command, turning on a sixpence as he cut corners, keeping his balance and covering the ground and fences with deceptive ease.

'Oh!' Laura gasped in alarm as the horse knocked one of the bricks in the wall with a hind foot. The block teetered on the edge but stayed in place, drawing a sigh of relief from the crowd.

'He took a whole stride out there!' Fiona cried as Black Diamond cleared the penultimate fence and Declan turned him on an angle for the final obstacle. 'Go on, Declan!'

Laura didn't know whether to laugh or cry when the round was over.

'Look at the time, Fiona, they were ages inside it!' she exclaimed, jumping up and down with excitement.

'The last one will have to go some to beat him, sure enough,' her friend remarked.

'I can't watch!'

Fiona laughed.

'Here they come.'

Suspense

The woman riding the bay gelding into the ring looked far older and more experienced than Declan and Laura remembered she and her horse had completed an inch perfect round last time. She crossed her fingers, hardly daring to breathe, as the woman urged the horse forward at breakneck speed.

'She's faster,' Laura fretted as the pair reached the halfway stage. 'Oh, Fiona!'

Her friend gripped her hand.

'Don't worry.'

Laura couldn't help it! They cleared the wall with ease and approached the final three fences, still ahead on the clock. Then they were clear with two fences to go. The arena was hushed with rapt anticipation.

Laura felt ill when the rider also took a stride out and the last but one fence was cleared with ease.

But wait! The woman made a tactical error and cut the corner more sharply than Declan had done. Too sharply. The angle was too tight and it was impossible for the horse to make the fence. It balked, ducking out to one side.

Laura wanted to cheer with relief as the woman, her chance of victory gone, turned a circle and presented her horse at the fence again, this time clearing it.

'That'll be three faults for a refusal, so she'll drop back,' Fiona exclaimed in satisfaction. 'Declan did it, Laura! He's won!'

The next hour or so passed in a blur. The horses and riders came back in to collect their prizes and then did a lap of honour, cantering round the arena to the delight of the cheering crowds. Declan led the way, the winner's rosette flapping from Black Diamond's bridle.

The commentator announced then that Declan and Black Diamond had qualified for the prestigious final in Belfast in a few weeks' time, and Laura thought she would burst with pride.

It was dark when they finally congregated at the lorry to prepare for the journey home. Jack was quietly satisfied with his charges' performance. Laura tried not to get in the way, longing for the moment she could talk to a flushed and smiling Declan.

Soon Black Diamond, rugged and bandaged, was safely loaded and assorted tack and gear stored in the various cubby holes, ready to go. Jack walked round to the driver's door and climbed in, switched on the lights and started the engine.

Laura moved forward to climb in, but Declan appeared behind her, taking her arm and holding her back so Fiona was next to climb in the passenger door beside her father.

'Up you go,' Declan teased, lending her a helping hand up to the cab.

'Hey!' Fiona laughed. 'Give me a chance.'

'I'll go next,' Declan murmured, swinging himself swiftly into the cab and sliding along the seat.

For a moment Laura hesitated, uncertain, wondering if Declan really wanted to sit next to Fiona. Then, as she climbed in and found herself snuggled closely between Declan and the door, a new warmth percolated through her.

In the shadows inside the cab, neither Fiona nor Jack noticed as Declan's left hand snaked out and took Laura's right one, fingers entwined.

As the lorry eased towards the exit, joining several others in the queue to leave, her thigh pressed gently against Declan's.

Fiona chattered incessantly, unconcerned that no-one was paying much attention to her. Laura was conscious only of Declan beside her, talking to her softly, excited at his win and delighted to have qualified to ride in Belfast.

'You were fantastic,' Laura whispered to him. 'It was so exciting. Thank you so much for asking me.'

'I told you you'd bring me luck!'

Daringly, she leaned against him.

'It's been such a wonderful weekend.'

'I'm pleased for you, Laura,' he whispered back, his breath fanning her cheek as he turned his head towards her. 'And pleased for me — now you won't have to go away.'

Laura smiled in the darkness, hugging the knowledge to her.

'What's Happened?'

Too soon, they reached the outskirts of Killarney and Declan's fingers squeezed hers in silent reassurance.

Life seemed just about perfect. Surely nothing could go wrong?

But as they approached the entrance to the hotel driveway, where Jack had promised to drop her off, Laura gasped, her eyes widening in alarm. Light poured from the windows and spilled across the driveway. Two police cars stood outside and people were milling about.

'What on earth is going on?' Jack exclaimed, halting the lorry.

Fear gripping her, Laura scrambled from the cab and ran towards the building. She saw her parents, white-faced, climbing into one of the police cars. Her grandparents stood anxiously on the steps, holding tightly to a tearful James.

'What's happened?' Laura demanded breathlessly, watching as the police cars sped away down the drive, gravel spraying from the wheels.

'Oh, Laura.' Tears in her eyes, her grandmother stepped forward. 'It's Luke. He's missing, love.'

'Luke missing? How? Why?'

Her gran put her arm round Laura's shoulders and pulled her close.

'He was terribly upset by something that happened in the park earlier today. He ran off. They're organising a search party. So far no-one's been able to find him.'

10

A Waiting Game

'Dan, what on earth are we going to do?' Kathleen cried. 'Luke has always been so sensible. He's never done anything like this before.'

Dan took his wife in his arms, and held her tight, her face ashen with a mix of fear and pain.

'They'll find him, Kath.'

'What if they don't?'

'We can't think like that. Everything will be all right, you'll see.'

He could only pray he was right. But the wait for news seemed endless. It felt like hours since the Garda had brought them to the park, to the place from which Luke had disappeared. Now, staring out into the inky darkness, Dan's stomach clenched in fear for his son. He felt so useless. If only he could join the search! But he knew he would be more hindrance than help.

Kath pulled away from him and walked to the window, wrapping her arms around her. He felt unable to comfort her.

It was at times like this he most regretted the accident which had robbed him of his physical strength. He was letting his family down. Earlier he had been euphoric about the bank's agreement for upgrading the hotel, but all that paled into insignificance now.

Turning, Kath saw the frustration and discomfort on her husband's face. Not only was this as terrible for him as for her, but he needed his medication, and to be somewhere comfortable.

'Dan, I think you should go back to the hotel for a while.'

'No,' he disagreed vehemently.

'Laura and James will be worried sick, not to mention my parents. Don't you think . . . '

'I'm not leaving you.' Dan's jaw set in stubborn determination. 'I need to be here when they find Luke.'

Kath shook her head, unable to argue.

'At least sit down for a while to rest your back. I'll send someone home for your pills and some food.'

'But . . . '

'Please, Dan. We both have to be strong. I need you, too. And I'm worried you'll do yourself more harm if you don't take your medication.'

'All right.'

With obvious reluctance, Dan complied.

She watched him for a moment, sharing his pain. After a quick word with the policeman who waited with them, their needs were organised. Kathleen returned to her vigil by the window, willing those searching for Luke to find him sooner rather than later.

'Luke! Luke, answer me!' Stephen listened for a sound, but there was none. He had never felt so terrified in his life.

'Luke?' Beside him, Annie's torch beam swept from side to side, casting eerie shapes and shadows. 'Luke, where are you?'

'I have to find him, Annie!' Stephen cried.

'This is all my fault!' His throat was hoarse from shouting; fear tightened his chest.

'No!' Annie turned to face him, gripping his arm, her eyes fiercely determined in the torchlight. 'No, Stephen, you are not to blame.'

'I'll never forget the horror on his face, Annie.' He groaned, reliving the day's events.

The call had come in that Sunday morning about a badly injured red deer stag up on Torc Mountain. Stephen had set out immediately, taking another ranger with him. They had searched for a couple of hours. When they had found the deer, it was clear straightaway that the kindest thing to do was save him further suffering. It was Stephen's responsibility, but he never enjoyed taking a life. He closed his eyes; the hated sound of the gunshot echoing across the mountain reverberated in his mind.

When they had finally driven down to meet Annie at the visitor centre by Muckross House in the afternoon, the body of the majestic animal in the trailer behind them, he'd had no idea that his parents had brought Luke to the park to find him.

The boy had run up to them, taken one look at the dead deer and at the gun in his uncle's hands, and his face had crumpled, tears of shock and rage spilling from his eyes.

'How could you?' he'd cried. 'You're supposed to care for things, not kill them. I hate you! I hate you!'

Before anyone could stop him, Luke had taken off at a run. Now it was dark, and while Kathleen and Dan waited, distraught, for news of their young son, the Garda and park staff were out searching.

So far, no-one had seen or heard any

sign of the boy. The authorities were talking about calling the search off until dawn. But even if it meant he had to stay out here all night alone, Stephen refused to give up until Luke was found.

'I'll never forgive myself if anything has happened to him.'

Annie's hand brushed his face.

'Stephen, it is not your fault. Please don't do this to yourself.' She held the torch between them, illuminating their faces.

'Come on, Luke needs you now. We can help him. You know this terrain better than anyone. Let's go!'

Stephen ran a hand distractedly through his hair and closed his eyes. Annie was right. Luke needed him more than ever now. There would be time to explain when he was safe again.

'Take Care'

Nodding, Stephen looked down at Annie, sensing her concern in the darkness.

With a tired smile, he dropped a hasty kiss on her mouth.

'Thank you.'

'So, what's the plan?' she challenged briskly, keeping him focused.

He took out his walkie-talkie and called in to base.

'It's Stephen. Nothing yet.'

'OK,' a disembodied voice crackled back. 'We have people out in the arboretum, round Castlelough Bay and along towards Brickeen, ahead of you. Others are checking round Muchross again and moving out round Dundag Bay towards Kilbeg Bay. We're still discussing calling it off until daylight. Over.'

'Thanks. But I'm not coming in until Luke is found. Annie and I are heading into Reenadinna.'

Stephen was adamant — finding Luke was his responsibility.

'Are you sure?' The voice was surprised.

'Take care in there.'

'Will do. Out.' He secured his radio

and took Annie's hand in his as they prepared to enter the dense woodland. 'This way.'

He hoped to goodness Luke hadn't come in here, but the boy had last been seen heading in this direction. Stephen knew that few people were as familiar with this area as he was himself.

The yew wood was a unique habitat, covering some sixty acres of the peninsula, near the meeting point of the lower and middle lakes. But there were reefs and fissures in the undulating outcrops of limestone which could be dangerous. Even during daytime, little sunlight penetrated the trees.

'Luke!'

They walked carefully, scanning with their torches, stopping regularly to call and listen. Stephen refused to give up, strengthened by Annie's constant presence and the reassuring pressure of her hand in his.

'Luke!'

They kept calling. It was dark, cold and difficult underfoot. Stephen had no idea how much time had passed when Annie suddenly tensed, her torch beam snapping back to a point on the ground to one side of them.

'Stephen! What's that?'

He hurried over and knelt down, retrieving the object from a crack in the ground.

'It's a shoe! I'm pretty sure it's Luke's!'

Hope and excitement gripped him as the light from their torches revealed recently disturbed earth.

'Wait here.'

Stephen moved forward with caution, his heart swelling when he saw the curled-up form of a small body. He hurried the rest of the way down the slope and crouched at his nephew's side.

'Luke? Can you hear me? Are you OK?'

The small body trembled, and a grubby, tear-stained face looked towards him.

'My ankle hurts. And I'm c-cold.'

'It's OK. You're safe now.'

'I'm sorry.' Luke sniffed, his voice wobbling.

Stephen hugged the boy to him, sending up a prayer of thanks.

'Don't worry about anything now. Let's get you home. All right?'

Luke nodded, burrowing against him. Stephen swallowed the lump in his throat, his voice hoarse.

'Annie?'

'I'm here,' she called from above. 'How is he?'

'Not too bad. A bit scared, and he's hurt his leg. I'm going to have to carry him. Can you come down and collect the stuff?'

'Sure.'

Moments later she had slithered down the slope and rested beside him. She slid an arm round his shoulders in a reassuring hug. Stephen smiled, his gaze holding hers for a second in the shadowed torchlight.

'Hi, Luke.' Annie gently switched her attention to the boy.

'We can radio back once we're out of this cover,' Stephen announced, receiving nothing but static in his attempts to contact base. 'I think we should crack on.'

Annie nodded.

'I'll take your pack.'

Handing over his things to her, Stephen rose to his feet, Luke clasped safely to his chest. The boy wound his arms round his uncle's neck.

'Come on, young man. Everyone will be very relieved to see you.'

Moving On

'Sam, there's a phone call for you,' Brian announced, coming into the busy workshop. 'It's your dad. You can take it in the office.'

Ducking out from under the bonnet of a car, Sam frowned.

'My dad?'

He wiped his hands on a clean rag and headed towards the office. He'd only spoken to his parents on Saturday night. What had happened to make his dad ring now, on Monday morning, while he was at work?

Time To Come Clean

Avril smiled reassuringly as he entered the office and gestured to him to use Brian's desk.

'Dad? Is something wrong?'

'Everything is OK, Sam . . . now. It was too late to ring you last night, but we knew you would want to know.'

Sam listened in amazement as his father related the tale of Luke going missing in the national park and the search to find him.

'Is he all right?'

'A bit shaken up. He's sprained his ankle but he's otherwise unscathed. He'll be running around again before we know it. James, however, is disgusted as he's been sent off to school, while Luke spends the day in bed!'

Sam laughed.

'I can imagine. It must have been dreadful for you and Mum.'

'Pretty grim for a while, but we're fine now.' It was clear from his dad's voice he was trying to make light of a frightening experience. 'All OK with you, Sam? I'm sorry about you and Nicola.'

'It was the right thing for both of us, Dad. I'll fill you in at Christmas,' Sam promised.

'We're looking forward to seeing you. Now, I'd better let you get back to work.'

'Sure. I'll speak to you at the weekend. Love to everyone.'

As he hung up, Brian returned from the workshop. Seeing the couple's concern, Sam explained what had happened to his younger brother.

'That's dreadful. What an ordeal for them.' Avril clapped a worried hand to her mouth.

Brian nodded his agreement.

'But they are all OK?'

'Dad said everyone's fine.'

'It must be upsetting for you, all the same.' Avril frowned. 'You must feel so far away, I mean.'

Sam wondered whether now was the time to grasp the nettle and break his news to them.

'Actually, I did want to talk to you about that.'

'Is something wrong, Sam?' Brian prompted.

'I'm really grateful to both of you for the chance you've given me — and all you have done for me personally.' He paused, smiling self-consciously. 'I feel bad because I've done a great deal of thinking and I'm really not sure that I belong here.'

'You miss your family.' Avril's words were more statement than question.

'Yes,' he admitted. 'More than I ever expected. But, to be honest, I don't want to let you down, either.'

Brian gave him a friendly pat on the back.

'You're not doing that, Sam. You've

worked very hard and we appreciate it. However, you need to decide what is best for you. Have you made any plans?'

'I have.'

Grateful for Brian and Avril's understanding, Sam outlined his hopes for the future.

'You've certainly been busy.' Avril smiled. 'Your parents will be proud of you.'

'Thanks. I hope so. I want to keep it a surprise until I go over at Christmas.'

'And you won't be coming back.' Brian finished for him.

Sam nodded.

'I've been offered a place in January doing mechanical engineering at college. If it's OK with you, I wondered if I could give notice to work up until Christmas week?'

'We'll be sorry to lose you, Sam.' Brian's smile reflected disappointment and respect.

'Indeed we will,' Avril agreed. 'But if you've had a change of heart, it's better to decide now. Let us know in the meantime if we can do anything.'

'I will. Thank you.'

Sam went back to work, his heart a whole lot lighter. The sooner he was reunited with his family the better.

★ ★ ★

'Is everything all right with you and Luke now?'

'Yes, thank goodness.' Stephen smiled at his mother and accepted the cup of tea she handed him. 'We had a long chat about things the other day and I explained how sometimes culling is necessary when an animal is sick or injured. I think he understands.'

Mary Fitzgerald stirred a spoonful of sugar into her own drink.

'Your da and I felt so responsible. Three weeks on, I still have nightmares about what could have happened.'

'It was no-one's fault, Ma. Luke's fine now — and he's learned a valuable lesson.' He reassured his mother, remembering his own fears, and the joyous smiles of relief on Kathleen's and Dan's faces when he carried their son back to them.

'Poor boy, I hope it won't put him off being a ranger.'

'He's very young yet.' Stephen helped himself to one of his mother's freshly-baked ginger biscuits. 'Where's Da?'

'He's away doing something with James before he drops him off at the hotel.'

'They seem to have taken to each other.'

'That's so, right enough.' His mother looked up, her eyes twinkling. 'And is your Annie settling in to living with you?'

'Ma, she is not my Annie, and she's not living with me,' Stephen protested, trying to hide his irritation.

'What would you call it then?'

He frowned, not fooled by her innocent smile.

'Look, it just makes more sense than her being out at the hostel during the winter, that's all.'

'Sure — if you say so!'

As his mother chattered on, Stephen stared out of the window in his parents' kitchen at the view of the hills and lower lake. He had to be mad. While half of him was delighted to have Annie in his home, the other half couldn't understand what had possessed him to suggest it. He had always valued his privacy. He'd never asked anyone to move in before. So why now?

Why Annie?

Stephen shook his head. These were questions he still couldn't answer. It wasn't as if their relationship had progressed very far — if you could call it a relationship. He'd only kissed her a couple of times. But he smiled at the memory, admitting that yes, he did want to kiss her again — although Annie wasn't an easy person to read and he wasn't certain where he stood with her.

She had been a rock of support while Luke was missing. Somehow he had to convince her that he cared for her.

He glanced at his watch and realised he'd have time to cook something special for supper to surprise her when she came home. Finishing his tea, he washed his mug and kissed his mother goodbye.

'I have to be going, Ma.'

'Look after that girl now!'

Chance Encounter

'Hello, Annie!'

Drawn from her contemplation of the supermarket shelves, Annie swung round to see the friendly barmaid from Buckley's pushing a trolley towards her.

'Jess! I'm sorry. I was miles away.'

'I'm like that myself when I'm shopping,' Jess agreed with a grin. 'So, how are you doing?'

'Fine, thanks. You?'

'Grand. How are things with Stephen?'

Annie fought the blush that threatened to stain her cheeks.

'Pardon?'

'You've settled in at the house?'

'Oh! Yes, I have. It's more convenient than the hostel,' Annie continued, wondering what people were thinking about her new living arrangements.

Jess smiled in encouragement.

'Better company, too!'

'Well . . . ' Annie broke off, embarrassed, her flush deepening at the teasing.

'Stephen is such a great guy,' Jess chattered as they walked along the aisle, continuing their shopping. 'I went to school with him, and so did my husband, Kieran. Stephen was best man at our wedding five years ago. I'm so pleased you're together. He's been so much happier since you've been around.'

Annie stared at Jess, amazed at what she had heard.

'We're not actually together. Stephen and I are just friends,' she stressed. Her emotions in an unexpected tangle, her traitorous thoughts led her to wonder what it would be like to really be with Stephen . . .

'Oh? Are you sure?' Jess's disappointment was clear. 'I had so hoped he had found someone. He's not really dated since Easter — not after Roisin . . . '

'Roisin?' Annie cut in, curiosity getting the better of her.

Jess glanced round to see they were alone and lowered her voice.

'Dreadful woman. Attractive, but honest to goodness, Annie, she made Stephen's life miserable. All his friends were glad when she moved on to pastures new in Dublin. Now you've come along!' She grinned again, clearly undeterred by denials of a budding romance.

And what of Stephen, Annie wondered? Was he glad this Roisin had moved on from his life? Or was he still carrying a torch for the woman his friends disapproved of?

A Certain Something

The questions, along with an invitation to join Jess and Kieran for dinner one evening, filled her thoughts as she made her way home a little later.

Stephen was in the kitchen when she went in to put away her shopping.

'Hi.' He looked up and smiled warmly as she entered.

'Hi. Something smells nice.'

'I thought I'd try out my speciality on you.'

'Oh! I wasn't expecting you to wait on me all the time,' Annie exclaimed. 'I ought to take a turn.' She was well aware he had done the bulk of the chores since she had moved in.

'It's fine, Annie.' He poured her a glass of wine. 'I enjoy it.'

She accepted the drink with a shy smile.

'Thank you. Have I time for a shower?'

'Sure, no problem.'

She hurried upstairs, the smile still on her face, and busied herself with a quick shower and change of clothes. In the time she had been here, Stephen had been an easygoing and gracious housemate. She felt uniquely comfortable with him. But she also felt something else . . . something she had tried hard to hide . . . even from herself.

Annie looked at her face in the mirror before going back downstairs. A slight flush coloured her cheeks and there was a shimmer in her eyes. Embarking on any kind of relationship had been the farthest thing from her mind when she had left Canada.

But the evening stretched ahead, and Annie had the notion that anything could happen . . .

'Do you think they'll like them?'

Kevin smiled down at his young grandson's anxious face and ruffled his hair.

'Of course, James. Everyone will love your presents.' James watched as his grandad stowed the packages in the boot of his car.

'And you'll look after them for me until Christmas?'

'Sure, I will.' Kevin tapped the side of

his nose and winked. 'Just between the two of us.'

'Our secret!' James grinned.

The smile remained on Kevin's face as the boy chattered happily on the journey back to the hotel. He'd enjoyed spending more time with his grand-children since Kathleen and Dan had moved to Ireland. He loved them all, but he'd formed a special relationship with James these last few months.

Retiring from the hotel and moving to the bungalow with Mary seemed to have given them both a new lease of life. If everything worked out with the hotel refurbishments, Kathleen and her family should secure their future and he would be a very contented man indeed.

'Did you manage all your errands?' Dan asked, as James bounded into the kitchen ahead of his grandfather.

'It's a secret, so I can't tell you.'

'Of course. Silly me!' Dan shared a smile with his father-in-law. 'Do you want to take some biscuits upstairs and get on with your homework?'

James grimaced.

'If I have to,' he grumbled.

'That was the deal. Luke's already up there.'

'OK.' After grabbing a handful of cookies, James gave his dad and his grandpa a quick hug and ran up the stairs.

'I hope he wasn't too much of a handful.' Dan smiled again.

'He was fine. I enjoy spending time with him.'

'Can I pour you a drink?'

Kevin placed a hand on his shoulder, preventing him from getting up.

'I'll help myself.'

'It feels so strange around the place, now we're closed for the renovations,' Dan admitted when Kevin joined him at the table.

'I can imagine. When do the workmen start?'

'On Monday. Fortunately, much of the work seems to be cosmetic rather than structural. Hopefully it will all run smoothly and we can start taking bookings again for the end of February.'

Kevin frowned.

'Do you mind if I offer a bit of advice?'

'Of course not. I'd welcome it.'

'Knowing builders as I do, I'd recommend you don't take too many firm bookings for February in case the work does over-run. You don't want to have to cancel and put people off,' he explained. 'It's better to be a bit short for a week or two than create bad faith.

'If I were you, I'd work from March and Easter for bookings, to allow for anything unforeseen.'

'That makes sense. It's easy to get carried away and be too ambitious,' Dan agreed, considering Kevin's opinion.

'It will be grand when it's all done. I don't think Mary and I ever realised how shabby things were becoming.'

'That's often the way when you are in the midst of it, though,' Dan sympathised.

'True enough. But we feel bad, Dan. We've landed you with so many difficulties.'

'Please don't, Kevin. Neither Kath nor I feel that way about things at all.' Dan's voice was sincere. He met his father-in-law's gaze and gave him a rueful smile. 'Things may not have gone as smoothly as we'd planned, but that's life, isn't it? We still did the right thing coming here.'

'That's grand. Mary and I are over the moon to have you near us.'

'It's been good for us all — especially the children.'

Kevin finished his drink and smiled.

'Well, I'd best away home! Are Kath and Laura out?'

Dan nodded, folding up the plans for the refurbishment which he had spread all over the table.

'Laura is with Fiona, watching the Belfast Horse Show on television. Declan is competing there. And Kath has gone to town to do some shopping.'

'Give them my love.'

'I will. And thanks again for helping James.'

'No problem. We'll see you soon.'

Glancing at his watch after Kevin had left, Dan frowned. Where was Kath? He'd expected her back ages ago.

'I Don't Need Your Help'

Kathleen juggled her parcels and carrier bags as she headed for her car. She hadn't meant to be this late, but she'd met an old school friend and they had shared a cup of tea and some cake in a nearby café while each caught up on the other's news.

It was a relief not to have to worry about hotel guests and meals for a change! She imagined it would be chaos once the builders started work. Goodness only knew what Christmas would be like amongst the turmoil. Still, it would be wonderful to have the family all together to celebrate.

December was proving to be a busy month. Not only were there the upheavals at the hotel to contend with, but the children had various events at school — plays, concerts, football matches. But despite that, she was more sure than ever they had done the right thing in moving here and taking up this challenge.

'Oh!' She gasped in alarm. So absorbed had she been in her thoughts that she hadn't noticed where she was going.

Tripping on an uneven paving stone, she managed to save herself from falling, but her shopping scattered across the pavement. Annoyed at her own carelessness, Kathleen bent down and began to gather her things together.

'Let me help you,' a familiar voice offered.

She glanced up and met Liam's gaze in the glow of the streetlights.

'I can manage, thanks.'

'Kathleen,' he pleaded, ignoring the dismissal in her voice. 'Did you hurt yourself?'

'No. I'm fine, Liam. And I don't need your help.'

'You need it. You just don't want it.'

Her annoyance building, Kathleen ignored him and stood up with her bulky shopping bags. She marched to her car and tossed the carriers unceremoniously inside.

'Thank you,' she said grudgingly, accepting the stray bags he had carried for her and pushing them across the seat with the rest of the shopping.

'Kathleen, please . . . '

Slamming the car door, Kathleen turned to face him.

'What do you want, Liam?'

'We ought to talk.'

'I don't think we have anything to talk about.'

'Look,' he began, reaching out to detain her when she made to walk away, 'you're back here to live now. James is doing well — at my school. It's natural we're going to bump into each other. Can't we clear the air about the past and build some kind of civilised relationship?'

Kathleen shrugged him off, disturbed at being alone with him, unwilling to face old hurts and betrayals.

'No, Liam, I don't think we can,' she replied, refusing to meet his gaze.

'But . . . '

'Excuse me, please, I'm already late, and my family are waiting.'

Her hands were shaking as she unlocked the car door and scrambled inside without her customary elegance. She just wanted to get away. Why must she bump into Liam now? She had managed to avoid any encounters with him for months. He made her as uncomfortable now as the day they had parted so acrimoniously, all those years ago. Why on earth did he want to rake up the past?

He stood in front of her, palms flat on the bonnet, blocking her departure. Starting the car, Kathleen inched forward, forcing him to stand aside.

'Kath . . . ' he began.

'Goodbye, Liam.'

'This isn't over,' he called out as she made to drive away. 'We have unfinished business, Kathleen.'

11

An Invitation

'Don't come any closer,' Fiona warned. She was propped up in bed, her voice croaky and full of the cold. 'It's bad enough me missing the school concert.'

Laura smiled sympathetically.

'Poor you. How are you feeling?'

'Rough,' Fiona admitted, reaching for a tissue as she succumbed to a fit of coughing.

'I'll leave you to rest. Get better soon. You're all coming to us for Christmas next week.'

'Try and keep me away. Especially if your Sam is flying over!'

Laura grinned at her friend's response. Clearly the 'flu hadn't robbed Fiona of her sense of humour.

'You're terrible!'

'Is your mum still acting weird?'

347

Laura's grin faded and she frowned.

'She's been really stressed out since the building work started. We're all keeping out of her way.'

Fiona started coughing again and Laura decided it was time to leave.

'I'd best go. I'll look in on you again soon.'

'Thanks for the magazines. I've been so-o-o bored,' her friend croaked, waving her off.

Downstairs, Laura lingered to make a fuss of Podge, the sturdy Labrador, who lounged in front of the range, his tail beating a tattoo on the floor.

'Off for your riding lesson?' Fiona's mother asked with a smile as she came into the kitchen. 'Declan's waiting for you.'

'Thanks, Mrs Har . . . Auntie Teresa.'

Laura hoped there was no tell-tale flush staining her cheeks at the mention of the young man.

She pulled on her boots and hurried across the yard to the stables, where she found Declan tacking up Fiona's dark grey gelding, Frosty. Laura had gained confidence after her nervous start and progressed well with her riding. Fiona now insisted she rode the livelier horse.

'Hi,' she breathed.

Declan turned with a smile.

'Hi, yourself. How are you?'

'Fine, thanks. Still buzzing after watching your performance in Belfast on TV. You were great!'

'I made a silly mistake in the jump-off.'

'But you came third out of the whole of Ireland in your first major season!'

His smile widened at her praise.

'Yes. I know. I'm that chuffed! Sorry, I shouldn't be such a grump.'

'You're not,' Laura replied loyally. She met his gaze, her heart thudding under her ribs. 'Are you sure you have time to do this now?'

'I'm secretly glad Fiona is laid up so I can spend some time alone with you,' he confided, his voice dropping to a conspiratorial whisper.

Laura glowed with excitement at his admission. But as they walked towards the indoor school, her nervousness increased. Compared to Declan, she was still a novice on a horse. Would he think she was awful?

Securing her hat, she scrambled clumsily into the saddle.

'Just ride round to warm up and get used to the feel of him again,' Declan advised, walking to the middle of the school and watching as she urged Frosty first round one way and then changed rein to circle the other way.

Over the next half-hour, Declan put her through her paces and Laura soon forgot her nerves. He was a patient tutor who made the lesson fun. And he was generous with his praise.

'You're a natural, Laura.' He smiled as he called her to halt in front of him. 'You're doing grand. You looked really good out there.'

Trial And Error

Flushed from the exercise and his compliments, Laura smiled back.

'Thanks.'

'Do you fancy trying a small jump?'

'Oh!' She frowned, uncertainty gripping her. 'I don't know ... I've not done that before.'

'Just a tiny one, to see how you feel.' He walked across to set up a low pole for her.

Oh, help! Laura watched silently, anxiety turning her insides into knots.

Declan came back to check her stirrups and her grip, and gave some final words of advice.

'Lean your weight forward over his withers as you approach the pole and let him do the work. OK?'

'I'll try.'

It felt as if a whole flight of butterflies was fluttering in her stomach as she stroked Frosty's neck before urging him forward.

'Circle round until you feel ready,'

Declan called out. 'Just go over the pole from a trot to start with.'

Plucking up the courage, Laura guided Frosty towards the jump.

A couple of strides out, the horse broke into a canter of his own accord and, although she did as Declan said and leaned forward with Frosty's movement, his jump was far springier than she had anticipated. With a cry of surprise, she lost her balance and landed with a thud on the dirt floor.

'Laura?' Declan rushed to her side. 'Laura, are you hurt?'

'No, I'm fine.' She waved away his concerns, determined not to lose face.

Declan's hands steadied her as she straightened up. He helped brush her down and she stilled. His eyes met hers, then he lifted a hand to her face, softly stroking her cheek with the pad of his thumb. Laura sucked in a breath, her skin tingling.

'You had a smudge on your face,' he explained softly.

Laura couldn't speak. She could do

nothing but stare at him, her heart pounding. Declan's eyes darkened and stepping even closer, he tilted her head and lowered his mouth to hers. She'd never been kissed properly before. It was wonderful!

Just as she wished she could stay in his arms for ever, he let her go.

Could she remember how to breathe? Laura dragged in a lungful of air and let it out again in a rush, her body trembling.

'Come on, up you get and try again,' he urged, giving her a leg up.

'But . . . '

'No buts. Did you not know there's an old saying that you have to fall off a hundred times to be a good rider?'

She smiled at his teasing.

'You must be sore, then!'

'And you have ninety-nine to go.' He grinned back. 'Trust me, you can do this. Take your time. Try and keep to a trot this time.'

Success

Still buzzing from Declan's kiss, Laura gathered the reins and her concentration and trotted round a second time. Taking a deep breath, she held Frosty in at a controlled pace, headed towards the pole, and, found herself and the horse still together on the other side.

'I did it!'

'Well done!' Declan grinned, coming across to congratulate her. 'It wasn't the most elegant jump I've ever seen but it was a jump.'

'Can I do it again?'

'Not today. Always end on a good note. I want you in one piece for Christmas.'

'Are you not going home to Dublin for the holiday?' she asked breathlessly as she dismounted.

'No. I'd rather be here.'

Christmas suddenly looked even more exciting.

'Fiona and her parents are coming

down to us for the day. Will you come, too?'

'Won't your parents mind?'

'No, not at all.' Laura crossed her fingers behind her back, thinking of her mother's strange mood. 'Please say yes.'

Declan grinned, taking her hand in his.

'Of course, yes! Thank you.'

Her heart was throbbing fit to burst — Laura couldn't wait for Christmas Day!

* * *

'Are you sure your family won't mind me coming for Christmas Day?'

'Annie, for goodness' sake!' Stephen exclaimed, amused and exasperated in equal measure.

She wrinkled her nose and he smiled.

'I'm sorry, it's just . . . '

'Just what?' Stephen crossed the gap that separated them and took her hands in his. 'What are you worrying about?

Didn't Kathleen say after the midnight service last night that everyone was looking forward to you joining us?'

'But it's a family day,' Annie protested, unable to voice her concern that she had only been invited because it was Irish hospitality and they felt sorry for her being on her own.

'It's also a day for friends and for sharing.'

'Yes, but . . . '

An Unexpected Guest

An insistent ring of the doorbell forestalled further discussion. Stephen ran a hand through his hair and sighed.

'Can you get that, please, while I finish these presents?'

'Sure.'

Annie left the kitchen, a mix of relief and regret swirling inside her. She knew she had upset Stephen with her doubts, but had been unable to explain what was really on her mind.

Pushing her uncertainty away, she opened the front door and was startled by the sight of a spectacular redhead, wearing an expensive leather jacket.

'May I help you?' Annie asked hesitantly.

The redhead smiled.

'I'm here to see Stephen.'

'Oh, of course.'

Annie stood back to let the woman in, unease unfolding inside her.

'He's in the living-room.'

'Thank you.'

The redhead swept gracefully down the hallway. As they entered the room, Annie stood awkwardly to one side, watching Stephen as he glanced up. His eyes widened as the newcomer stepped confidently towards him.

'Hello, Roisin. This is a surprise.'

'A nice one, I hope.' She smiled coolly, moving in to kiss him briefly. 'Happy Christmas, darling.'

'Thank you. You, too.'

Annie's heart lodged in her throat at the exchange. So this was the infamous

Roisin she had heard about — the woman Stephen had loved but of whom his friends had disapproved? Tall and exquisitely beautiful, it was easy to see why the assured redhead would gain any man's attention. What a contrast to herself!

Annie glanced down grimly at her own comfortable clothes; her outfit seemed drab compared to the flamboyant Roisin's.

Her gaze clashed with Stephen's and misery lanced through her as he made the introductions.

'Annie, this is Roisin, an old friend of mine. Roisin, Annie is from Canada and working in the park with us for a while.'

'Hello.' Annie's reluctant response barely made it past her lips.

'Annie.'

Roisin's frosty gaze dismissed her in a millisecond. Annie cringed. Jess had told her this woman had made Stephen's life miserable, but was he still carrying a torch for her? He certainly

358

didn't appear upset to see her.

'How is Dublin?' Stephen asked as he continued wrapping the twins' presents. 'Everything you hoped?'

'It would have been better if you had come with me,' Roisin purred, setting Annie's teeth on edge.

Unable to bear another minute, Annie mumbled an excuse and ran upstairs to her room. Roisin's appearance had hit home with stunning vengeance. Despite her reservations, her determination not to get involved again, she had fallen for Stephen, big time. But how could she possibly compete with someone as glamorous and self-assured?

Whatever his friends said, Stephen had obviously been attracted to her at one time — he had loved her. Whatever had caused them to part, may not have ruled out the chance of a reconciliation. Why else would Roisin be here?

Annie glanced towards the open door. The murmur of their voices downstairs floated up to her.

Feeling annoyed at herself, Annie swiped crossly at a tear that trickled down her cheek. She was a fool to think that a good-looking, warm and funny man like Stephen was ever going to be interested in someone like her. She certainly couldn't spend Christmas with him and his family now. She was sure he'd only been drawn into taking her in the first place after pressure from his mother and Kathleen.

'Annie?'

Stephen's voice startled her.

'Yes?'

'Get a move on, it's time to leave.'

'You go without me,' she called back, her voice stilted and distant.

She sucked in a breath when she heard his footsteps on the stairs. Hastily, she brushed away the last of her tears and resolutely kept her back to him as he walked into her room.

'What's wrong, Annie?'

'Nothing,' she lied. 'I just don't feel up to it, that's all.'

Sensing him move closer to her, she tried to step away, keeping her face averted, but he caught hold of her arm.

'Whoa! Wait a minute. Come here.' He drew her towards him, frowning as he cupped her face and saw the evidence of her tears. 'What's this for?'

'Nothing,' she fibbed again, a tremor running through her at the touch of his hands.

'It doesn't look like nothing to me.'

Annie raised her hands to his wrists, intending to push him away.

'Stephen . . . '

'Tell me,' he insisted. 'Please.'

'I just feel I'd be in the way,' she whispered.

Stephen's frown deepened.

'Why would you think that?'

'I'm sure you'd rather take Roisin,' she replied, lifting her eyes to meet his.

'Then you couldn't be more wrong. Is Roisin's visit what this is all about?'

'Partly,' she admitted.

Shaking his head, Stephen studied her for a moment, the pads of his thumbs brushing the remaining moisture from her cheeks.

'Yes, Roisin was on her best behaviour today. And, yes, she comes in a beautiful package. But she's not the one for me . . . I've explained that to her.'

'You have?'

'No-one has ever lived in this house with me but you, Annie. Doesn't that tell you something? I guard my own space jealously. But I wanted *you* here. I gave up my privacy for you — not Roisin, not anyone else. Only you.'

'Oh,' Annie whispered, barely able to force the word past the lump in her throat.

Stephen shifted, his body pressing hers gently against the wall as he brushed her hair back from her face, one finger tracing the line of her brow.

'You, Annie, are warm and genuine

. . . and very lovely,' he told her gently.

'I am?'

'Absolutely. I'm probably rushing things, but I've never felt this way about anyone before.'

Annie had no idea what to say. Which was just as well, she smiled to herself, as Stephen closed the gap remaining between them and she surrendered to the magic of his kiss.

'Annie, if you don't want to spend Christmas with the family that's fine. We can just drop the presents off and come home.'

'No! That's not what I meant,' she protested in alarm. 'I just didn't want you to feel you had to include me.'

'Don't be daft,' he scolded.

'But . . . '

Stephen tilted her face up to his.

'Annie, how much clearer do I have to be? I want to spend my Christmas with you.'

Annie smiled, the last of her doubts evaporating.

'Then I'd be delighted to come.

There's no-one else I'd rather spend the day with, either!'

Shared Confidences

'Can I come in?'

Laura glanced round as Sam opened her bedroom door.

'Sure.'

'Are you ready? Mum sent me to fetch you,' he explained, flopping on the bed and watching as she brushed her hair and applied a little lip gloss.

'Everyone's here.'

'OK.'

'Including Declan,' he teased, smiling at the blush that washed his sister's cheeks.

She put away her make-up and swung round, her tone defensive.

'So?'

'I think he's nice, Laura.'

'Do you?' She attempted nonchalance, but her breathless voice and sparkling eyes gave her away.

'He makes you happy!'

'He's cool.' She couldn't help herself confiding in her older brother. 'I've never felt like this before, Sam. Do you really like him?'

'I do. He helped me bring some more logs in and we had a chat. We both like music and football. I don't know one end of a horse from another, but Declan said he didn't know anything about car engines. We agreed we were just interested in different kinds of horsepower!'

Laura laughed, hugging him.

'I'm really pleased you got on.'

'We're going to be good friends, Declan and I.' He returned her hug warmly, knowing how anxious she was.

'I hope Mum and Dad like him.'

'Stop worrying.' Sam stood up and took his sister's hand. 'Let's go down.'

'Do I look OK? Declan's only seen me in riding gear or school uniform.'

Casting his gaze over her slender figure in a strappy red dress, Sam realised how much she had grown up.

'You look beautiful,' he told her honestly.

'Really?'

'Truly. He's a lucky guy.' Sam hesitated a moment.

'Take care, OK? Don't rush things,' he added protectively. 'Now,' he whispered as they walked along the landing, 'tell me about your friend, Fiona.'

'Like what?'

'Is she seeing anyone?'

'No.' Laura giggled. 'But I know she likes you. She was over the moon when she heard you'd be here this week!'

He'd be here a lot longer than that, Sam thought to himself.

'I think you and I are going to have a very happy Christmas,' he confided as they walked down the stairs to join the others.

This is the best Christmas ever.' Teresa sighed as she sank, replete, on to a sofa in the sprawling family sitting-room.

'Kathleen, you did us proud with that

dinner. I don't think I'll ever move again!'

A chorus of approval echoed her sentiments, drawing a smile from Kathleen.

'Thanks, I enjoyed it all — and I had a lot of help from everyone, even the twins,' she teased, recalling their chaotic efforts at decorating the over-dressed Christmas tree which now listed dangerously in the corner of the room.

Silence descended as one by one they dozed off the after-effects of their traditional Christmas meal. Kathleen closed her eyes, delighted at how well everything had gone, and how happy everyone seemed.

Stephen and Annie couldn't stop looking at each other, she reflected. She was glad Stephen was happy. He'd had a close call with the awful Roisin.

Her parents were contented, too. This was the first Christmas in goodness knew how many years that they hadn't been rushed off their feet.

It was great having Sam over for the

week. It completed the family. He didn't seem to be suffering any ill effects from his split with Nicola. Indeed, Kathleen thought, opening her eyes and watching as he and Fiona gathered up the remains of the wrapping paper, it seemed he had found a new interest.

She looked round the room and realised Laura and Declan were missing. A frown creased her brow. Declan was a lovely young man. She liked him. But she hoped Laura wasn't getting in too deep. Her daughter was still young, although there was no doubt she had grown in confidence and maturity these last few months.

Kathleen could hear the twins playing outside with the Harringtons' dogs, Podge and Nell. Where did those boys get their energy?

She yawned as she relaxed in front of the open fire, its warmth and comfort seeping into her. Dan had taken Jack and her father upstairs to look over the renovation work, so she could sit for a moment and forget the clearing up.

Only one issue refused to go away. It lay festering in the corner of her mind — Liam. Ever since her unfortunate meeting with him, she had been on edge. The family had noticed her erratic behaviour and had been treading on eggshells around her. But resolving things meant facing Liam.

A Creeping Concern

Kathleen shook her head. She wouldn't allow worries about the past to spoil this special Christmas.

Dan came into the room, her father and Jack following behind. She managed a smile for him as he came across and perched on the arm of her chair, leaning awkwardly to kiss her.

'That was a great meal,' he said.

'I think everyone enjoyed it.'

'Of course they did.' Dan laughed. 'Look at them!'

Kathleen smiled at the prostrate

bodies littering the room.

'Dan, do you know where Laura and Declan are?'

'In the kitchen doing the washing-up.'

'You're kidding?' Surprised, she struggled to sit up. 'I'd better go and help.'

His hand on her shoulder held her in place.

'Leave them alone, love. They're enjoying themselves. He's a really nice boy. I don't think we have anything to worry about there.'

'I hope you're right.'

'I am. But if it makes you feel better, I'll go and check on them in a while.'

'There is a dishwasher, you know,' Laura remarked, swirling the pan scraper through the soapy water.

'Now you tell me!' Declan teased, tossing aside a wet tea towel and taking a clean one to dry the big roasting tin she had just handed him. 'This is more fun, though.'

'If anyone can ever call washing-up 'fun' . . . '

'It is if we're doing it together.'

Warmth stained Laura's cheeks. Declan always made her feel special — as if spending time with her was all he wanted to do. She looked up at him and smiled, emboldened by the warmth in his eyes.

'I feel like that, too.'

'Good.' His fingers stroked her face. 'You're so pretty, Laura. Thank you for asking me to share your Christmas.'

'You being here has made it the happiest ever. And I love my presents,' she added, fingering the gold horse necklace he had given her, along with a book.

'Thank you for my CDs.'

His eyes darkened as they gazed into hers and excitement flickered through her as his lips met hers.

'Can I Ask You Something?'

The sound of voices and footsteps on the stairs intruded and they broke

371

apart, smiling at each other before they turned back to their task.

'Do you think your parents would let me take you to the New Year dance?' Declan asked.

Laura smiled.

'I should think so.'

'I'll ask then — if you'd like to come with me, that is?'

'Of course I would!' she enthused, then she saw his mischievous expression and realised he was only teasing. Laughing, she splashed him with water. 'If you're serious, talk to my dad.'

They chattered on about all sorts of things as they finished off the washing-up and were laughing together as her father came into the kitchen.

'Hi.' He smiled.

'Hi, Dad. Are you OK?'

'Fine, sweetheart. Thanks for doing this, you two. You shouldn't have bothered.'

'It wasn't any trouble, Mr Jackson.' Declan grinned. He set down the last of the dishes and folded the used tea towels for the wash. 'And it was the least I could do, given your hospitality and that fantastic food!'

Dan nodded.

'We're very glad you could spend the day with us, Declan.'

'Thank you. It's been grand.'

'That's us done.' Laura beamed, struggling to undo the knot in the ties of the apron she had put on to protect her dress. 'Oh, bother!'

'Here, let me.'

Dan watched as Declan deftly helped her, releasing the knot and then solicitously taking the apron from her and hanging it back up. He was impressed with the young man's courtesy and the care he seemed to take in looking after Laura. If the happiness on his daughter's face was anything to go by, she appreciated it, too.

'Where is everyone?' she asked now, turning to her father, her pretty face flushed and alive.

'In the family-room.' Dan smiled and gave her a brief hug.

Laura skipped ahead of them out of

the kitchen and Dan turned to follow, hesitating when Declan called him back.

'Mr Jackson?'

'Yes, Declan?'

'Can I ask you something?'

'Of course.' The young man looked nervous and Dan's heart went out to him, remembering how he had felt at that age. 'What is it?'

'There's a dance at New Year. I'd very much like to take Laura. Would that be OK?'

Seeing the anxious play of emotions in Declan's brown eyes, Dan smiled, feeling deep inside he could trust him with his daughter.

'I'd be happy for Laura to go with you . . . especially if you'd agree to take Sam along,' he added, curious to see how the boy would react to the small test.

'That would be grand, Mr Jackson! Thank you!' Declan grinned enthusiastically. 'And I'm sure Fiona will be coming, too.'

They walked together to join the rest of the gathering. As they entered the family-room, Dan saw Laura sitting on the rug by the fire, stroking the dogs. Her gaze turned to the doorway, anxious anticipation in her eyes. He didn't know what messages her young man was sending, but Dan winked at her and was rewarded with such a beaming smile that it brought a lump to his throat.

'Right!' Teresa announced, clapping her hands for attention. 'Forget what I said earlier, I'm getting my second wind! It's time for some party games!'

Amidst the general groans and laughter, Dan crossed to Kathleen's side and squeezed her hand. This had, indeed, been the very best of Christmases.

★ ★ ★

'We won!' Fiona exclaimed, jumping up and down with excitement, holding her orange aloft in triumph. 'We did, didn't we, Uncle Dan?'

'You did, Fiona, but I'm not so sure about the 'we'.' Dan held his hands up to stifle the protests of the losing teams. 'And it was almost fair and square!'

He'd sat out the pass-the-orange game because of his back, opting instead to referee the others' dirty tactics.

'I don't know about anyone else, but I'm gasping for a drink,' Kathleen commented, heading for the door.

'I wouldn't say no to a cup of tea,' Mary agreed, stifling a yawn. 'How about the rest of you?'

'I'm hungry,' Sam announced, stretching lazily.

'Me, too, me, too!' the twins chorused.

'You can't be,' Laura gasped. 'We ate enough at lunch-time to last a week.'

Shaking her head, Annie laughed.

'I'm with you, Laura.'

'Come on, guys.' Stephen stood up, rubbing his hands together, the twins tagging along behind him. 'Snacks in the kitchen. We'll leave the ladies to recover!'

'Cheek!' Teresa complained, grinning as her daughter rose to follow the others. 'I thought you wouldn't say no to food, Fiona!'

It was dark outside; a frost was beginning to crisp the grass and edge the branches of the trees in silver. Kathleen bustled about the kitchen, making sure everyone was happy and had what they needed. She smiled as Dan came in to replenish drinks and take a couple of cans of beer from the fridge.

'OK?' he asked, stopping for a brief kiss.

'Tired, but OK.'

'Leave the clearing up, love,' Dan urged. 'Come back and sit with us. The others will be going soon.'

They were just leaving the kitchen as the phone rang.

'Oh, who on earth can that be?' She tutted, waving Dan on as she turned back to answer it. 'Waterside Hotel.'

'Kathleen, it's Liam.'

Kathleen gasped in shock.

'What do you want?'

'Please don't hang up. I wanted to say I'm sorry for upsetting you. Just think about giving me a chance to explain — to clear the air.'

'I don't know . . . '

'Think about it,' he added.

'Merry Christmas, Kathleen.'

Liam hung up before she could respond. She set the receiver down and walked away, her emotions in turmoil. How dare he ring her now! How dare he spoil this wonderful day!

'Is anything wrong?' Dan asked, a frown of concern on his face.

She looked at him in bewilderment for a moment, then realised he meant the phone call.

'Oh . . . no . . . wrong number,' she fibbed. Disbelief and hurt flashed in Dan's eyes.

The incident dampened her spirits for the remainder of the evening. She tried to smile and join in, but Liam loomed large in her mind, as did the knowledge that she had lied to Dan . . . and that he knew. If only she had told him years ago what had happened. Now she had blown it up in her mind — probably out of all proportion . . .

'Well, Mary, my girl, I think it's time we were away,' Kathleen's father announced, drawing her from her reverie, amongst protests from the children. 'It's been a grand day, right enough.'

Bodyblow

Before they had time to rise and begin gathering up their things to leave, Sam stepped forward.

'Just before you go, I have something I want to say while we're still all together.'

'Is everything all right, son?' Dan quizzed. Kathleen frowned at the mix of emotions crossing their eldest son's face.

'Fine. More than fine, actually.' He

looked round at everyone and smiled before turning back to his parents. 'The thing is, I wanted this to be a surprise.'

'What do you mean?' Kathleen prompted when he paused, unable to stand the suspense, a strange awareness pricking at her senses.

'I've done a lot of thinking, as you know, over the last few weeks and I've made some decisions about my future.

'I've given up my job. Brian and Avril were great, but working there full-time made me realise it's really not what I want.'

Sam hesitated, suddenly uncertain. He met his father's gaze, took a deep breath and continued.

'I'm going to be starting an engineering course at college next month. In Killarney,' he added with a grin.

'You're moving home? To Ireland?'

'I am.' He acknowledged his mother's question, his grin still in place as he met the realisation and delight in Fiona's eyes. 'If you'll all have me. The thing is, I made enquiries when I was over last time and I hope to follow you, Dad . . . into the fire service.'

For some moments he was swamped with excited hugs. He'd been frightened his dad would be upset, but his pleasure was clear in his smile and embrace. As things quietened down, however, Sam realised his mother hadn't moved and was staring at him pale with shock.

'Mum . . . what's wrong?'

Kathleen blinked away her tears, realising all eyes were now focused on her, confused at her reaction to her son's news. But how could she bear it if what had happened to Dan, happened to Sam . . . or worse?

'Mum?' Sam spoke again. 'What is it?'

Kathleen rose shakily to her feet.

'I wish we'd never come to Ireland!' she cried.

Leaving the astonished gathering behind her, she turned and fled sobbing from the room.

12

Confession

It wasn't the most exciting New Year's Eve she had ever experienced, Kathleen reflected ruefully. She waved goodbye to Sam and Laura, who were off to meet Fiona and Declan for the dance, and closed the front door. Luke was on a sleepover at a friend's, and James was in his element staying at his grandparents' house. She and Dan were alone.

Kathleen leaned against the door for a moment, lost in thought. She still couldn't believe how badly she had behaved on Christmas Day. She had made peace with Sam easily enough. He had matured a great deal in the last few months and, although he understood her fears about the fire service following what had happened to his father, he was not about to be deflected from his goals.

She heaved a sigh and ran her fingers through her hair. Things hadn't been right between her and Dan since she had lied to him about Liam's phone call. There was a tension, a distance, and she didn't like it. She could blame no-one except herself so it was up to her to put it right.

She walked slowly through the deserted building to the family-room where Dan was sitting in a chair by the fire. There was no better time to start afresh than the end of one year and the beginning of another. She took a deep breath, applied a bright smile and crossed the room to sit beside him.

'Hi.'

He looked towards her warily, his expression guarded.

'Hi.'

'Can we talk, please?'

'If you wish.' Dan set his book aside with obvious reluctance. 'What about?'

Kathleen clasped her hands together

in her lap. This was going to be more difficult than she had anticipated.

'I've been very silly, Dan, I know that. I spoiled everyone's Christmas — especially Sam's. He knows I'll support him . . . I've explained.

'I just got so frightened something might happen to him, as it did to you. I couldn't bear that . . . not on top of everything else.

'But I can't wrap you all in cotton-wool, can I?' she finished with a harsh laugh as she fought away a sudden prickle of tears.

'I understand your fears, Kathleen,' Dan said quietly, failing to meet her gaze. 'But what happened to me was an accident.'

'I know. Just as I know Sam has to live his own life.'

Dan stared gravely at the flames dancing in the grate.

'You said 'on top of everything else'. What did you mean by that?'

'I don't know . . . the usual things . . . worrying about the children, you, the hotel — all sorts of things. I've let everything get on top of me . . . And then there's Liam Flanagan . . . '

Her words trailed off as Dan faced her, pain evident in his eyes.

'I wondered if we'd get round to Liam. I presume it was he who rang on Christmas evening?'

'Yes.' She swallowed nervously. 'Dan . . . '

'So how long has it been going on?'

Kathleen stared at him uncomprehendingly.

'What?'

'You and Liam.' Dan's voice was thick with hurt and bitterness. 'Not that I can blame you. I'm not much of a catch now, am I?'

'Oh, Dan! No! No, that's not what this is about! You've got it all wrong,' she cried, moving to his side and taking his hands in hers.

'Have I? He's always looking at you, ringing for you. And you've been acting so oddly.'

Kathleen's heart broke as she listened to her husband's anguish. Why had she

385

been so foolish? How long had he been torturing himself . . . imagining the worst?

The tears that had earlier threatened now trickled down her cheeks.

'Dan, I'm so sorry. I've made such a mess of everything. It's not what you're thinking, I promise. I love you, Dan. Please, let me explain.'

He nodded, doubt and sorrow clouding his expression.

'Everybody . . . my folks . . . all my friends round here . . . they all think my parting from Liam was friendly,' she began, sitting back on her heels in front of his chair, her fingers still linked with his. 'But it wasn't.'

'Go on,' Dan prompted.

'I'd known Liam most of my life. I had a bit of a crush on him when I was at school, Da was right about that, and I was stunned when he asked me out. I was sixteen; he was seventeen — my first proper boyfriend. We went out for two years. We had fun, but I realised after a while that although I liked him a lot. I wasn't really in love with him. What I didn't realise was that Liam felt far more involved than I did.

'I was thrilled when I was accepted to do my nursing training in London. I couldn't wait to leave here. I've told you all that — how I wanted to see more of the world than just County Kerry . . .'

She broke off for a moment, trying to assess Dan's reaction, but his expression was inscrutable.

'Anyway, Liam was really upset when I told him I was leaving. I was too young and silly to appreciate how hurt he was. I think I saw him as just another shackle.'

Dan frowned.

'So what happened?'

'Oh, Dan, I feel so guilty, even after all these years,' she confided, a shiver running through her.

'You know how you can convince yourself that some things never happened? And then someone lights the touch paper and sparks it all off again . . . ?'

'Kath, you're not making any sense.' Dan's frown deepened. 'I don't understand. What are you trying to tell me?'

'We'd never rowed about anything. Liam was always so easy-going. Everyone liked him. He was something of a local hero — a sportsman.' She closed her eyes as she remembered that final night.

The pressure of Dan's fingers on hers drew her from her memories.

'We had a humdinger of a row about me leaving. I really hurt him, Dan. I said some horrible things . . . cruel things.

'Liam drove off distraught and had an accident. He wrote off his car and his leg was so badly damaged he was in hospital for months. He never told anyone what had happened, but I knew it was my fault.' She swiped away a tear that squeezed between her lashes.

'Oh, Kath.' Dan sighed and slipped his arm around her. 'You can't blame yourself. It was an accident.'

'But, I do, Dan. I always have. The

worst of it is, I've never had the courage to face him — to apologise to him.'

'And now?'

Kathleen shook her head.

'I hadn't seen or spoken to Liam since that night until you and I went to look over the school for James. It was such a shock coming face to face with him. I thought he'd hate me. I forgot, of course, that it's not in his nature.

'Remembering it all . . . how stupid and childish I was . . . I've been so ashamed, so worried about what people would think of me . . .

'But that's not the worst of it . . .

'Liam had planned a career in sport. He could have played internationally, but I robbed him of that. Seeing him as a head teacher, brought the consequences home to me.

'I know this must sound so foolish now — it even sounds foolish to me — but I was so busy trying to avoid him, that I was looking at things through the eyes of the eighteen-year-old I was, instead of the woman I am.'

'Forgive Me?'

Dan dropped a kiss on the top of her head, relief tangibly seeping from him as he held her close.

'We all do silly things, Kath. We all have regrets and we all make mistakes.'

'I knew things had got out of hand when I behaved so badly at Christmas. I rang Liam this afternoon, while you were out with the twins. It turns out he wanted to apologise to me!' she told him with a teary laugh. 'How stupid is that?

'Anyway, he doesn't blame me. He's really enjoying his career and he's getting married in the summer! He just wanted to clear the air.'

'I don't know what to say.'

After a long moment, Dan tipped his head back, eyes closed.

'Can you forgive me for ever doubting you?'

'Darling, please, there's nothing to forgive. If I hadn't been so stupid, I would have realised how strange and furtive my behaviour must have seemed.

'If I'd just been honest and confided in you this would never have happened.'

Dan gently brushed away the remaining tears.

'I've been just as foolish, love. I've been consumed with worry that I am failing you all because I'm not the man I was. But pride stopped me confiding in you.'

'Don't ever say that,' Kathleen implored. 'You're all I need, Dan. You're the person I love most. Nothing will change that.'

She slid her arms around him. This had been a painful lesson, but a valuable one, she realised, vowing to be more open in future.

'I love you,' he whispered, his lips finding hers.

Snuggled together, Kathleen felt closer to Dan than she had in a long time. Their relationship had been tested but had survived and, she believed, strengthened.

They were still curled in each other's

arms when the clock struck midnight.

Her fingers gently tracing the face of the man she loved, Kathleen cupped his face in her hands and kissed him.

'Happy New Year, darling!'

'It will be, Kath.' Dan smiled, holding her tight. 'It's time to leave the past where it belongs, Kathleen. Let's look to the future.'

★   ★   ★

'Laura Jackson, what can I do for you?'

Rising from the chair outside the school office, where she had been waiting since the last class finished, Laura met Sister Philomena's kindly gaze and smiled shyly.

'I wondered if I could have a word with you, Sister.'

'Of course, my dear, come away in with you.' The nun beamed, bustling inside to sit at her desk.

'Sit down, sit down. Good. Now, are you having any problems?'

'Oh, no, Sister. I'm really enjoying being here.

'I don't want to bother you, but . . . '

Sister Philomena tutted.

'Now, now, my dear. Tell me, please.'

'I've been thinking about my future,' Laura began. 'I know the rest of the class take the Junior Certificate this year and I was wondering if you think I am too far behind with the work to be able to pass the written exams in June?'

'But you're not behind at all, Laura! Whatever gave you that idea? You've made excellent progress since you joined us. All your teachers are delighted,' the headmistress enthused.

'Thank you, Sister. Only . . . the thing is . . . I think I'd like to go into teaching; geography, possibly.' Laura looked up and saw only encouragement in her headmistress's eyes, inspiring her to continue.

'If I work hard, do you think I'd be capable of that?'

Sister Philomena's face creased in a happy smile.

'More than capable. I think you'll make a grand teacher. You're a clever girl, Laura, but just as importantly, you have a gentle heart and kind nature. If this is the way you are leaning, we'll do all we can to help you.'

'Thanks!'

'I'll look out some information for you and we'll talk again,' the headmistress promised. 'Away you go, now. It's wet, getting dark, and I think you'll find there's a young man waiting for you!'

Her cheeks flushed with happiness and embarrassment, Laura hurried from the office, collected her things and went outside to find Declan.

'We Need To Talk'

'How did you get on?' he asked, taking her heavy bag with one hand and reaching to twine the fingers of his other hand with hers.

'You were right, it was fine! And Sister Phil thinks I'll have no problem achieving my goal.'

'That's grand!' Declan turned to kiss her, before he slid his arm around her shoulders and held her close as they walked on towards the hotel.

Laura snuggled against him, happier than she had ever been.

It was already well into January. Since Christmas, time had flown by, taking Laura with it in a romantic whirl. Declan had been spending more and more time at the hotel with her and Sam. And recently he had taken to meeting her after school and walking her home.

'We need to talk, Laura,' he said now, snapping her out of her reverie.

His serious tone alarmed her.

'What about?'

'Us.'

'Oh.' Doubts and fears tumbled inside her, her earlier happiness toppling like building blocks. 'You don't want to see me any more?'

Declan halted, turning her to look at him, her face pale in the gathering dusk.

'Of course I do, silly! Where did that come from?'

'I just thought . . . '

'Laura!' He hugged her, stroking her hair. 'It's not that at all. But we do need to discuss things. I have some news.'

'What is it?'

'Are you cold? No? Then let's sit for a while now the rain's stopped.'

Declan led her through the hotel grounds to a covered bench that overlooked the shimmering waters of the lough and the brooding, mountain-ous backdrop.

He spread his coat out on the seat and Laura sat beside him, wondering what all this was about.

'Declan, is something wrong?'

'No. It's just . . . I really care about you, Laura — a lot.' He turned to face her, holding her hands in his. 'I want to be with you. But first you have to finish school.

'I think ambitions are important. You want to be a teacher and . . . well . . . my dream is to be a successful rider. It's something I've wanted since I was small.'

'Of course. I understand.'

The Chance Of A Lifetime

Declan took Laura's hand in his.

'The thing is, Jack has just told me that I've been chosen to spend a year schooling with one of the top show-jumping trainers in Germany. It means I'll have to move abroad for a while.'

'I see.' Laura bit her lip, tears stinging her eyes. Not to see him for such a long time . . .

'That sounds like an amazing opportunity,' she said bravely.

'It is. I'll have the chance to compete on a much bigger circuit and learn so much. Jack wants me to take Paprika, so we'll train together. He has the next Olympics in mind.'

Laura could see how much it meant to him, and yet she felt desolate at losing him.

'You have to go, Declan. You can't turn a chance like this down.' She tried to hide the wobble in her voice.

'Oh, Laura.' His fingers tightened on hers. 'A year is a long time at our age. I can't ask you to wait for me.'

'You're not. I'm choosing to.'

He raised one of her hands to his face and pressed a kiss against her palm.

'When do you go?' Laura asked shakily.

'Not until after Easter. You will keep in touch, won't you?' he whispered.

She nodded, laughing through her tears.

'Sure. They have e-mail, don't they? We can write and stuff — we could even get one of those webcams.'

'I'm going to miss you, Laura.' Declan drew her into his embrace.

At least he wasn't giving her the brush-off as she had feared. In fact, it seemed he was serious about her. Well, Laura thought philosophically, if it was meant to be, it would be. In the meantime, they'd better make the most of the weeks they had left.

They walked back to the hotel hand in hand and she tried to reassure herself that this year would go just as quickly as the last. Who would have thought last Easter that her family would be living a new life in Ireland? Whatever the future held in store, she and Declan had something special.

★　★　★

'I just knew you and Stephen would be good together.' Jess grinned, her expression smug. 'Didn't I say that?'

'You did,' Annie agreed, slipping on her coat and waiting while Stephen brought the car round.

Kieran draped an arm around his wife's shoulders.

'And isn't she just insufferable when she's right?' He laughed.

Jess poked him in the ribs.

'That's enough of that!'

'Thanks for a lovely evening, both of you.' Annie smiled. 'We've had a great time.'

'It's been grand having you. You must

come again soon,' Jess insisted.

Annie said her goodbyes and raced through the rain to the car.

It was almost February — how the year was marching on!

She had been so contented, both professionally and personally, since Christmas that she had already made a bold move. But she hadn't mentioned it to Stephen yet . . .

Annie glanced at his strong, attractive profile in the shadows of the car.

'You're very quiet,' Stephen commented, flicking a quick glance in her direction.

'Just thinking.'

They were soon home and Annie went into the kitchen to make some coffee.

'Do you want some or would you rather have a beer?'

'Coffee will be fine, thanks.'

By the time it was ready Stephen had stoked the fire, so she carried their mugs through to the living-room.

He accepted his gratefully and patted

the sofa beside him.

'Sit here. Tell me what's troubling you.'

She allowed him to draw her against him and she nestled there, sipping her coffee and watching the flames come to life.

Everything she wanted was here with Stephen. She could no more leave him than stop breathing.

Watching the play of emotions across her face, Stephen frowned. Were things just too good to last? He'd shared more of himself with Annie than he had with anyone his whole life. Suddenly, he felt vulnerable.

'What are you thinking about?'

'The future, mainly,' Annie admitted after a pause. 'I can't believe I've been here half my time already. The months seem to have flown by.'

'I know.' Releasing her with a sigh, Stephen sat up and placed his coffee cup on the table. 'I've been thinking about the future, too. I've decided to apply for the exchange place in Canada.'

Annie's eyes clouded in shock and

disappointment.

'Oh!' she exclaimed.

Was that it? Just 'oh'?

'Don't you want me to come to Canada?'

'It's not that . . . ' she protested, turning to face him.

Stephen tried to pretend it didn't matter.

'It's OK,' he told her flatly.

'No . . . no, Stephen . . . ' Annie rested a hand on his thigh. 'You don't understand.'

'Understand what?'

'I don't want to stop you experiencing Canada, if that's what you want, but . . . ' She hesitated.

'But?' Stephen held her gaze, his emotions checked.

'I won't be there.'

Smarting, he turned away.

'I see.'

'I Want To Be With You'

'No, you don't.' Her fingers brushed his face. 'I won't be in Canada because I'll be here. I applied for the ranger vacancy in Killarney. I've been accepted.'

He stared at her in bemusement.

'You're staying in Killarney?'

'Yes. Do you mind?'

'Mind?' He shook his head, trying to banish a fog of confusion. 'Of course I don't mind! But why?'

Her shy smile turned his heart.

'Why do you think? I love it here. For the first time in my life I feel I belong, and . . . '

'And?' He waited, hardly daring to hope.

'I want to be with you,' she told him simply.

'Oh, Annie,' Stephen breathed. 'Do you really mean it?'

'If you'll have me.'

'Of course I'll have you!' Laughing with happiness and relief, he drew her back into his arms. 'You scared me,' he whispered. 'I thought . . .

'I need to get something!' Stephen exclaimed and ran up the stairs to his study, his heart pounding with emotion.

After a quick search he found what he was looking for and hurried back down again, smiling at the puzzlement on Annie's face.

'Would you really have gone to Canada for me?' she asked as he rejoined her on the sofa.

'I wouldn't go to Dublin for Roisin,' he reminded her. 'But for you, Annie, I would cross oceans and continents.'

'Stephen . . . '

'I was going to wait until Valentine's Day to do this.' He grinned, taking the small box he had collected from upstairs and opening it to reveal a stunning amethyst ring. As Annie's eyes widened in shock, he slid on to one knee before her.

'I love you, Annie. Will you marry me?'

Tears slipped between her lashes as she eased the ring on to her finger and she threw her arms round him.

'Oh, yes! Yes, of course I will. I love you, too.'

And with that she met and matched a kiss that left no need for words.

* ★ ★

Wrapped in a fresh new coat of white paint, Waterside Hotel gleamed in the early spring sunshine. Dan emerged from his workshop, where he had been putting the finishing touches to the wooden horse he had carved for Laura's birthday.

He stood for a moment, enjoying the feel of the sun's rays on his skin, smiling when Kathleen joined him.

'It's a lovely day, isn't it?'

'The spring seems to be arriving earlier.'

'It's the climate — and we had a kind winter, neither too cold nor too wet,' she agreed.

The lesser celandines had been out for some time and the willow catkins were open, soon to be colouring.

'Stephen said the ravens are thinking of nesting, and the redwings and fieldfares have gone. The Greenland geese will follow in a couple of weeks.'

'You really feel the changing of the seasons here.'

Dan breathed in the clear, fresh air, turning to look at their home and business, surrounded by trees and set against the stunning panorama of lakes and towering mountains.

'So, what do you think?'

Kathleen brushed some wayward strands of hair back from her face and followed his gaze.

'It's amazing! Even better than I'd hoped.'

'Your parents were thrilled, when they looked round after the builders left.'

'Da loved it.' Kathleen grinned. 'He said we'd hit just the right note between modern and homely.'

'I'm glad. That's what we wanted. Even the fearsome Ms O'Rourke from the bank was full of praise. She even smiled!' he joked.

'And have you looked at the bookings? They're pouring in! If this is a sign of things to come, we're going to be very busy when we open again next week.'

'It's grand. Although, to be honest, I'm a bit daunted by it,' Kathleen confessed. 'I've become lazy these last weeks!'

Arm in arm, they walked round admiring the outside of the building.

'Is everything ready indoors?' Dan asked, a glint in his eyes. 'Has Laura guessed anything?'

'Not a thing, but it's been hard keeping the twins quiet! Sam is watching them like a hawk and poor Laura is moping around, wondering why Declan hasn't called. It's been awful, not being able to put her out of her misery.'

Dan glanced at his watch.

'It'll soon be time.'

'I can't wait to see Laura's face!' Kathleen beamed.

'Mmm. What a year! And what changes in Laura!' Dan laughed. 'I sometimes think she's fifteen going on thirty!'

'She's being very grown up about Declan going to Germany for the year, but you can see how upset she is. I'm so glad we agreed to let him do this for her today.' Kathleen smiled again, turning to face her husband. 'You were right all along about him.'

Two cars pulled noisily into the gravelled drive.

'Come on, your folks are here — and so are Teresa and Fiona. Let's go inside and hope the others aren't too far behind.'

Party Time

They entered the newly-refurbished building just as Sam came down the stairs with the twins, who were bursting with impatience. Laura was in the family-room and Dan felt a stab of guilt as she looked up, her eyes dulled when she scanned everyone coming in and realised Declan was not with them.

She couldn't understand it — he knew it was her birthday, but he hadn't even phoned! And when she had tried to ring the yard she had been told he had gone off on some errand. Why hadn't he told her?

And was it just her imagination . . . or was everyone acting weird today?

'Well, then, shall we attack the food?' Dan suggested, rubbing his hands together heartily. 'We can do the presents later. OK, Laura? You won't mind, will you?'

'Fine,' she mumbled sulkily.

Her mother had laid out an impressive buffet on the kitchen table and everyone helped themselves, carrying the plates back to the living-room, talking and laughing. Laura tried to eat but she wasn't very hungry. She fiddled with her food, frowning as the twins kept whispering together, looking at her and laughing.

The phone rang and her mother disappeared to answer it, returning after a moment and glancing at Dan.

Something was definitely going on . . .

'I'm stuffed.' Fiona sighed.

'We haven't had the cake yet,' Sam pointed out.

Fiona grinned.

'Well, I'll always find a corner for that!' she joked, making everyone laugh.

'I'll go and get it, then.' Kathleen slipped from the room with a mischievous smile.

'Close your eyes, Laura.'

Sighing, she did as her father bid. She wished they'd hurry up and get on with it — whatever it was.

She heard the door open again . . . a few giggles . . . people were moving about . . .

'You can open them now.'

That was Declan's voice!

Laura's eyes flew open and she gasped. He was kneeling in front of her with a beautiful chocolate Labrador puppy nestled in his arms.

'Happy birthday.' Declan smiled, settling the warm bundle in her lap.

'He's for me?' she whispered, hardly able to believe it. 'I can keep him?'

Everyone was grinning and wishing her a happy birthday. She looked at her parents, who nodded that it was really true, than back at Declan, before bursting into tears and hugging him.

'He'll look after you for me while I'm away,' Declan murmured. Laura didn't know what to say.

'Can I stroke him?' James pleaded, edging forwards. 'Ooh, he's lovely!'

'What are you going to call him?' Luke asked. The sleepy puppy yawned and stretched and licked Laura's face.

Unable to believe this was really happening, she wiped away her tears.

'Rolo. I'm going to call him Rolo,' she decided, bursting with happiness.

Kathleen sat beside Dan, choking back tears of her own as she watched her daughter's joy. The girl could hardly bear to let go of little Rolo to open her other gifts, all doggy things — toys, bowls, a collar and lead. Kathleen was so glad they had agreed when Declan had come to ask if he could do this for a birthday surprise.

She leaned back surveying the room; the people she loved. What a long way they had come.

Any day now it would be March, the hotel would re-open and Easter would be upon them. They had come full circle.

Kathleen watched her parents, happy and relaxed; they seemed years younger now the pressures of the business had been lifted from their shoulders.

The twins had grown and flourished in Ireland. Sending them to separate schools had been a great idea. The boys had found their own identities.

As for Laura, well, she had blossomed into a delightful, sensible young lady, with a responsible and appealing young man of her own. She watched them together now, a smile curving her mouth. They were both so young. The next year would be hard for them. But it would be good if their bond survived their separation.

Her gaze moved on to Sam. He was doing well, settling better than he'd hoped at college and enjoying his new course. He'd found a good friend in Declan, and if the looks he exchanged with the irrepressible Fiona were anything to go by, romance was bubbling there, too.

Kathleen exchanged a grin with Teresa. They had shared some difficult moments, but she was delighted their friendship had been rekindled.

Stephen had never looked so happy and contented. Her brother had found someone very special in Annie — someone with whom to share his life. Their wedding next summer was planned for the anniversary of the day they had met and was eagerly looked forward to by the rest of the family.

'Happy?' Dan whispered, slipping his arm around her and drawing her close.

'Very.'

Sighing with contentment, Kathleen relaxed in her husband's arms.

These changing seasons had seen her family grow stronger. Deep in her heart Kathleen knew that they would weather the future together, whatever it might bring . . .

THE BOYS NEXT DOOR

Janet Chamberlain

When Ross Anderson and his lively nephews move in next door to Alison Grainger, it ends her well-ordered life — a life that doesn't include children. The noise is bad enough, but Alison becomes critical of Ross's method of childcare even as she becomes attracted to him. She becomes involved in their welfare despite herself. But when it emerges that the boys' grandmother has persuaded Alison to record Ross's progress with the children, the rift between them gets even bigger.

Other titles in the
Linford Romance Library:

SO NEAR TO LOVE

Gillian Kaye

Despite Emma's dislike of Mr Peirstone, schoolmaster in Ellerdale, she is forced to go to School House to look after his children. There she meets his son, Adam, and falls in love. But Adam's circumstances don't allow for marriage. Then Mr Peirstone dies unexpectedly and Emma goes to work for Dr Redman and his wife, Amy, in Ravendale. The doctor schemes to matchmake Emma and Adam . . . but can there ever be a happy ending for the young couple?